THE
SHEPHERD'S
Song

THE
SHEPHERD'S
Song

LARRY BARKDULL

DESERET
BOOK

SALT LAKE CITY

Library of Congress Cataloging-in-Publication Data

Barkdull, Larry.
  The shepherd's song / Larry Barkdull.
    p. cm.
  Summary: Joshua ben Levi, a young Judean shepherd, is in search of a miracle. His wife, Miriam, is expecting their first baby, but complications threaten to take the lives of both mother and child. In desperate need of God's help, Joshua journeys to the temple in Jerusalem to make an offering and to pray; on the way home he becomes one of the shepherds chosen to greet the Christ child on the night of his birth.
  ISBN 978-1-60641-150-6 (paperbound)
  1. Jesus Christ—Nativity—Fiction. 2. Shepherds in the Bible—Fiction. 3. Christian fiction, American. I. Title.
  PS3552.A6166S54 2009
  813'.54—dc22   2009024681

Printed in the United States of America
Worzalla Publishing Co., Stevens Point, WI

10   9   8   7   6   5   4   3   2   1

Chapter 1

IN A SHEPHERD'S HOME

My eight-year-old cousin Ephraim was panting hard and shaking when he found me in Shepherds Field. His message was one that I was loath to receive. "Miriam is bleeding again!"

I grabbed Ephraim by both shoulders. "What's happened?"

Before Ephraim could answer, my father, Levi, heard the commotion and sprinted toward us. "Is it Miriam?" The alarm in his voice measured the tension that our band of shepherds had shared over the past several days.

Ephraim's father, Reuben, joined us. He knelt beside his son and said, "Tell us what you know, Ephraim." Overwhelmed now by three anxious adults, the boy began to cry. Reuben gathered him into his arms and asked, "Who sent you, Ephraim?"

"Leah," he answered. Leah, my mother-in-law, had been looking after Miriam since I had left my wife in her care three days before. Miriam had showed some signs of improvement, but I had only reluctantly departed. Ephraim had been conveying messages concerning

Miriam's condition between Shepherds Field and our home in Beit Sahour ever since. The boy looked up at me; his eyes were wide, his breathing rapid and shallow. "You must come, Joshua. Miriam is bleeding!"

I shot a glance at my father. He took my staff from me and said, "Run, Joshua. Run, and we shall pray."

As I approached our home in our little Judean village of Beit Sahour, I heard Miriam cry out. No sound had ever jolted me as this did. I burst through the door and saw my mother-in-law, wide-eyed and frantic, alternating between holding her daughter and ripping strips of cloth, as if her occupation could stop the bleeding. My dear wife lay on a bed of red-stained linen, pale and weak.

"Joshua!" Miriam cried, stretching out her arms. I rushed to her and fell at her bedside. She gripped me as in a vise, her hands as moist and cold as clay. The odor of blood and perspiration hovered about her bed.

"I'm here." I tried to give her comfort, while owning none myself. I turned to Leah. "What is to be done?"

My mother-in-law hesitated to answer, her face taut with worry. Miriam squeezed my hand hard and groaned. Leah moved quickly to the foot of the bed and lifted the sheet to expose Miriam's legs. When I heard

Leah's shocked intake of air, I felt a thick lump form in my throat. Miriam cried, "Please help, Mother! It hurts!" She began to pant as she thrashed about on the bed.

"Talk to her, Joshua!" Leah ordered as she massaged Miriam's bulging stomach with olive oil.

"Everything will be fine," I said, trying to believe it myself. Miriam clenched her eyes shut, thrust her chin into her chest, and groaned, the bulging veins in her neck and forehead threatening to burst. I was terrified. I shouted to my mother-in-law, "Do something!"

Leah paid me no mind but continued to work feverishly. Then she gasped and cried, "No, no!"

"What?" I said.

"Her water has broken! The baby is coming!"

Miriam began to sob. "Oh, Mother, no!" Still clinging to me, her body racked with invisible pain, summoning all her strength to speak, she looked at me and said, "I am so sorry, Joshua."

"You have nothing to be sorry for," I tried to reassure her.

"No, you don't understand." She began to cry again.

"What do you mean?"

When Miriam could not answer, Leah said, "Two days ago the baby stopped moving."

Leah's words cut through me like a blade. Early in our marriage, Miriam had lost two other children not long after conceiving. We thought she might never conceive again. After three years of hope and faith, our prayers were answered, and Miriam found herself with child. But there would be no joy today; our joy had once again turned to misery. She had been with child for eight months and would apparently lose this child, too.

"Are you sure?" I asked Leah, hoping for another verdict.

Leah nodded and turned away. Miriam pulled me toward her. "Joshua, I have felt nothing." Her eyes brimmed with tears. "Can you forgive me?"

I put a finger on her lips and hushed her. Tears spilled from my eyes as I gazed at my precious wife of seven years. We had grown up together in marriage; our mothers had been fast friends since before we were born, and our betrothal had cemented the ties between our families.

Since I had last seen her, only days before, my beautiful wife appeared to have aged markedly. Her smooth, olive complexion was tight and sallow. Her soft chestnut hair lay limp and matted. Always delicate and petite, she now seemed dangerously thin—except for her distended stomach, the dominant feature of her small body.

Leah coaxed Miriam's legs to a relaxed, flat position

and began washing them with warm water. I asked her, "When will she give birth?"

Leah shook her head. She answered with a list of disjointed facts. "She is so weak. Her labor has only begun—that could mean hours. But her water has broken—that could hurry things. She's bleeding—that's not good. The child isn't due for another month. It must be small . . . but then it is likely—"

"Dead?" I finished her sentence.

Leah closed her eyes and nodded. She confessed, "I do not know when Miriam will give birth, but if she hasn't done so by tonight—" Once again, she could not complete her sentence.

Miriam gripped my hand and cried out again, "Oh, help me!" She writhed in pain and rolled to her side, drawing her knees up, holding her protruding belly. Once again I made a vain attempt at comfort, when three women burst through the door and rushed toward Miriam. One of them was carrying a birthing chair with a hole in the seat.

In Beit Sahour, these women came at moments of crisis or birthing. No time for formalities. No time for pleasant greetings. They hurried across the room. A sudden rush of air followed them, making the house suddenly cool. Apparently dangerously cool. Leah ordered me to close the door. When I had obeyed and turned back, I saw that the women had joined Leah in buzzing about Miriam with urgent purpose.

Esther, an ancient, leathery woman, sat next to Leah and helped her tear strips of cloth. "I had hoped that the bleeding had stopped," she announced to all within earshot, apparently without considering that her statement might worry rather than console the patient. Miriam shot me a look of distress. As I moved toward her, Esther directed a question to Leah: "When did it start again?" At Esther's query, the other women looked up in anticipation of Leah's response.

"Just before dawn," Leah answered. Then pausing as if to weigh her response, she added, "Maybe a little earlier." She turned her head away and began to weep. Esther set aside the cloth and held Leah close. Watching the scene, I felt my anxiety increase. Tears were coming more easily now. They spilled down off my cheeks and onto the earthen floor. The other women were equally shaken. If someone needed to remain strong for Miriam today, all of us were failing at it.

"You didn't sleep at all last night, did you?" Esther asked Leah. Her appearance betrayed the answer. Her eyes lay sunken in dark circles of weary flesh. Her hands trembled. The wrinkles in her face had deepened overnight, carved into her forehead as with a knife.

Miriam groaned, arched her back, and began to breathe shallowly. The women reacted with experienced encouragement and instruction. I rushed to my wife and took her hand again. At this point, I cared not for custom. Birth was women's work, and according to the Pharisees, my mere presence in the same room could render me ritually unclean. But my wife's life hung in the balance. Nothing short of an act of God could cause me to desert her now.

When the episode had passed, Esther shot Leah an urgent, questioning look, and Leah responded, "Miriam's labor started last night . . . and her water broke just before you arrived."

One of the women released an audible gasp. Esther shook her head. "Too soon. Too soon."

Esther's words struck me hard. She pointed a bony finger at me and ordered, "Not enough light, Joshua. Get more lamps." Only one lamp was burning in the house. It was positioned adjacent to Miriam's bed on an overturned bushel measure. It gave off scant light, barely enough to distinguish the interior of our home, a single square room the length of two men.

Leah helped me. "There are two small lamps on the

shelf above the tools and grain." I located them quickly, filled them with oil, and set them above Miriam's bed. Immediately, the glow of the flames cast a sympathetic warmth over the cold interior of the house. The women hustled about without much talk, laying out instruments, lamb's wool, sesame and wild beechnut oil, pulverized saffron, bowls of warm water. One woman prepared a compress with a warm rock and gave it to Miriam to press against her stomach.

When my wife cried out again, I rushed to her, pushing aside the woman closest to her. I dropped to my knees and took her hand in both of mine, trying in vain to convey my strength to her. Miriam clenched my hands and groaned. The contraction was of such severity that it caused great beads of perspiration to form and stream down her face.

Miriam turned to me with the eyes of a frightened fawn. I had never seen this expression. It was more than fear; it was profound, desperate terror. As a shepherd, I was regularly called upon to fight off predators and guard the sheep with my life. At such times when a misstep could have landed me in the grave, I too had experienced fear; but I had never known terror until this moment. My courage plummeted; I was not as brave as I had imagined.

I looked desperately up at the women—first at Leah, then at Esther, and then at each of the others. I searched their faces for hope but found none. Leah took me by the arm and pulled me to the far side of the room. "You're in the way, Joshua," she said firmly.

Her harsh pronouncement was one that I was not willing to accept. "I can help," I protested. Leah shook her head slowly, and I realized that she was right. I glanced at my young wife, groaning in pain, blood continuing to soak the bedsheets. Esther and the other women were bustling about with skills I knew I did not have. I said, "I just can't leave her. I love Miriam. She's all I have." The words caught in my throat.

Leah embraced me. "I know how you feel, Joshua, but you really must leave. Let us work with her."

I drew in air, trying to compose myself, and then slowly let it out. My voice quavered as I asked, "Can you promise me that all will be well?"

Leah responded with tears. Realizing that she could make no promise, I began to crumple to the floor. She caught me and said, "For Miriam's sake, we must be strong. Each of us must do our part."

Resigned, I said, "Tell me what to do and I will do it, but don't ask me to wait outside and do nothing."

Leah gazed at me with great affection. She had known me from the moment of my birth. I was the only son of her dear friend, my mother. In a scene not unlike this one, Leah had attended her when I was born. In the process, my mother had hemorrhaged and sacrificed her life to give me mine. My father, Levi, had never remarried. Now Leah placed her hands on both sides of my face and forced me to look at her squarely. "We will do everything we can for Miriam. But what she needs today is beyond the skill of midwives. Miriam needs a miracle." She paused to allow her words to sink into my soul. "Do you understand, Joshua?" she asked, enunciating each word.

The weight of her question crushed me. I tried to answer yes but choked on my response. Leah gripped me securely and stared up into my eyes. My mother-in-law was a small woman, reaching me no higher than midchest. Nevertheless, she held me firmly.

I shifted my gaze to Miriam. Another contraction seized her, and with it came more blood. The activity of the women intensified. Leah turned me around to protect me from the scene. This is all wrong, I thought. Had not Miriam and I entered marriage with the hope of every couple of our tribe: to live into our old age in love, bearing and rearing sons and daughters unto God? If this

10

child had lived, we would have named it *Rachel* or *Joshua*. Was it possible that I might lose everything today—both my wife and our child? O God, take me, too! I gazed at my beloved, failing wife and repeated Leah's words in a whisper, "Miriam needs a miracle."

Leah nodded and relaxed her grip. I crossed the room and once more knelt beside my wife. Despite the desperate activity and gravity of the situation, I had not fully allowed myself to think that I might lose her today. Miriam turned her face toward me. Perhaps she perceived the worry in my eyes because at that moment she began to caress my face as with the touch of an angel. Nevertheless, her hands were trembling. She forced a smile. I tried to return it. I kissed her softly on the forehead and placed my face against her cheek. Leah and the women retreated a pace, as if they were witnessing something sacred.

Miriam suddenly reeled from another contraction, and the women raced to her. Esther attempted to move me, but I resisted. I looked up at her pleadingly. She nodded and backed away. I held Miriam's hand as if I were clinging to a drowning person. She squeezed her eyes shut and began to breathe rapidly, more perspiration gathering on her brow and face. The woman at the foot of the bed indicated a fresh flow of blood, and Esther shook her head sadly. Leah sat alongside her daughter's bed and stroked Miriam's hair. The third woman nervously sang a hymn while mixing a remedy in an earthen bowl.

Their efforts seemed so inadequate. Miriam appeared ghostly pale, weak, and shaking; looking at her, I knew that when I left I might never see her alive again. When the contraction diminished, her breathing slowed, but she had been exhausted by it. She looked at me and began to apologize again. "The baby—"

I hushed her. "Nothing matters except you." Our eyes met in the way that only two people who have become one can understand.

She whispered, "I know how much our child meant to you, Joshua."

Leah brushed back her daughter's hair and said, "Don't try to talk. Save your strength."

Miriam shook her head. "No, I have to say this to Joshua." She refocused on me, touched my face with a hand, and drew me close. "I know your faith," she said. "I know that you love God, and I know that He loves you. Go to Him now. Ask Him to help us."

I wanted to respond bravely, but I could not. I assessed her faith in my ability to prevail upon God, but I knew my weaknesses. I felt inadequate and power-less. "I am only a simple shepherd," I protested. "I am not a person of consequence. I have no great capacity to approach God."

"I believe in you," Miriam assured me. "I believe that you can ask God and He will hear you." She winced, took a deep breath, and gripped my hand until the pain had passed. She added weakly, "Remember what your father says: 'God will bless us today.'"

I knew the saying; I had grown up with it. My father was not a rabbi, but he knew the law of Moses well. He loved to impart his wisdom in proverbial form, and his favorite expression was also Miriam's:

> *God created today for us,*
> *To live and to love—*
> *In the safety of His fold,*
> *God will bless us today.*

That verse had rung true with my wife. She repeated it often and had formed a philosophy around it. Often, when she found me worrying, she would ask me, "Have we been blessed today?" Assessing our circumstances, it usually wasn't hard to find that God had indeed blessed us. Miriam was always quick to point out how God had blessed us *today*.

She was correct, of course; we always had enough food, enough shelter, enough clothing, enough love—

enough of everything, despite our humble circumstances. We were blessed by God, day by day. Now, squeezing my hand, Miriam said, "I believe in you, Joshua. I believe that you can ask God and He will hear you. God will bless us today." She urged me to repeat with her the words of the proverb: "God will bless us today."

When we had recited the verse, Leah nudged me to move. I kissed my sweet Miriam on the forehead, stood, and threw my cloak over my tunic. Springtime in Judea's hill country could be cold and wet. After I had adjusted my turban, I moved toward the door, but I could not make myself open it.

How could I leave her? Only her sending me on an errand to plead with God could have torn me from her. I knew what I had to do; and more, I knew that it was all I could do. It was what Abraham had done when he had been faced with an insurmountable obstacle. It was what all the holy prophets had done in the midst of their impossible situations. I would make my way to a high place, up to the holy temple in Jerusalem, the house of God. There I would approach the God of my fathers and offer up the prayer of my life.

And expect a miracle.

Chapter 2

SHEPHERDS FIELD

I hurried through the grassy pasturelands, last night's rain soaking my leather sandals. The morning sun shone on the meadows that comprised Shepherds Field.

My purpose was to choose a lamb from the flock and take it to Jerusalem as an offering. My religion taught me that I could not approach God, especially on a matter as critical as my wife's life, without making an offering. But I had another reason for going to Shepherds Field. My father would be there, and I needed him now. Before I journeyed to Jerusalem today, I would seek his counsel and his strength.

As I put more distance between Beit Sahour and me, I glanced northward toward Mount Hermon and imagined that its high snow fields were melting. I hoped Judea would soon shake loose from the grasp of an unusually cold and wet winter. The new grass, emerging wild flowers, and the arrival of newborn lambs heralded the beginning of spring.

Within the previous month, lambing season had ended at Migdal Eder on the outskirts of Bethlehem,

15

and recently we shepherds had led our flock back to the meadows near Beit Sahour. The move, somewhat premature for the season, had been calculated to provide me quick access to my wife in anticipation of the birth of our child. But on this springtime day which should have held so much promise, I had no cause to rejoice. I might hear the bleating of newborn lambs in the fields, but I would not hear the sound of new life in Beit Sahour.

I picked up my pace, urgently needing to find my father and then hurry to the temple to pray.

When I came within sight of the meadow, I scanned it for my father but did not see him. I knew the area well; I had been raised here. I headed toward a point on the north ridge covered with olive trees. That was the place where we tended our flock.

We shepherds were seven in number, most of us from the same family: my father, five others, and me. If my child were a son and if he were to live, he would have become part of this group, a thought that tortured me now. For as I climbed the ridge, I knew I could not save him; but I hoped that if I could get to the temple in time, I might be able to petition God to save his mother.

Breathlessly, I approached the scattered grazing flock. Standing guard was my uncle Reuben, Ephraim's father, a heavily bearded Goliath of a man, dressed in a striped woolen tunic the color of earthenware. Hearing my advance, Reuben instinctively raised his staff. I called out to him, "Uncle Reuben, it is I."

"Joshua?" Reuben peered through the morning mist. When he recognized me, he set his staff back upon the ground. I knew from painful experience that if I surprised him, he might fell me with a single blow of his staff or a rock from his sling.

As I drew closer, he said, "You startled me, Nephew." Then with characteristic concern he quickly asked, "Is Miriam going to be all right?" Despite Reuben's rugged appearance, he was a man of great compassion. I shook my head in answer to his question.

He frowned. "She's not well?"

"No," I answered. "Where is my father?"

Reuben gestured toward a nearby cave that we used as a shelter. I thanked my uncle and started for the cave. My quick movement troubled the flock, but with a word from me, the sheep settled down. I moved with purpose. No delay could be worth Miriam's death, and that was a possibility I could not entertain.

As I moved toward the shepherds' cave, I passed the sheepfold where my companions had bedded the flock the previous night. The sheepfold was in one of the many shallow limestone caves that dotted the landscape. Within a stone's throw was the shepherds' cave.

As I approached, I called out to my father, and presently, a sinewy figure emerged. Framed in the cave's entrance, my father stretched, pressing his hands into the small of his back, and winced. His body bore the scars of wounds that he had suffered while fighting off predators. Despite his age, he was still strong enough to rebuff a lion. When my father saw me, he hurried toward me. "What news do you have of Miriam? Is she bleeding again?"

I lowered my head and nodded.

He said, "We have been concerned since the moment Ephraim came for you. We have been praying all through the night."

My eyes became moist in a most unmanly way. "Last night Miriam's labor began," I said, choking out the words.

My father considered my words, and his question echoed Esther's concern. "It's too soon, isn't it?" When I didn't respond, he cleared his throat and asked, "And the baby?"

"The child has not moved for two days," I said.

My father began to pace. "Then we must pray much harder for Miriam."

"I know," I said, walking with him. "That is my purpose. Leah and the women are with Miriam." I struggled to say the words, each one an effort. "Miriam is very weak." When I couldn't continue, my father wrapped me in his arms and held me until I could compose myself. At length I dried my eyes and said, "Miriam sent me to pray." I gestured in the direction of Jerusalem.

My father understood. He said, "Nothing else could have torn you from her. Not now."

Once again tears were my response. Leaving Miriam had felt as if I were abandoning her, and turning away from her was certainly the hardest thing I had ever done. Only her request and our mutual hope that God might hear and answer my prayer of faith could have caused me to leave her.

I looked into my father's eyes and said, "When I left her this morning, she quoted your proverb: 'In the safety of his fold, God will bless us today.'" I paused as if to test the validity of the saying.

My father's expression spoke of a sudden realization that all his teachings hung on this moment. He put an arm around my shoulder and guided me away from the cave and toward the privacy of the pasture where the sheep were grazing. "It's more than a saying," he answered. "It came into my mind on the darkest and, remarkably, the brightest day of my life."

"The day you lost Mother?" I said, already knowing that my answer was correct.

Father nodded. "And the same day that I first held you in my arms." He guided me to the summit of the hill overlooking the meadow. As we walked he said, "I had imagined that I knew something about pain. It had been my companion for most of my life. As a child I lost my father, which forced me to become my mother's sole support. Later, I lost a sister to leprosy. Then I watched my brother die from the Romans' scourging, a small mercy that saved him from crucifixion. But the worst pain I ever felt was when your mother died."

I knew this part of the story; it had always made me feel as though I needed to apologize. I was alive because my mother had given her life to bear me, and the unhappy coincidence of Miriam's present condition did not escape me now. Perhaps my countenance dimmed when my father mentioned the recollection, for he quickly added, "On the other hand, I never experienced such joy as on that day." Facing me squarely, he said, "You are my greatest joy, Joshua." He held me in his gaze, not allowing me to look away; it was as though he intended to sear the sincerity of his statement into my soul.

When I offered a slight nod, he continued. "On that day, I took you here into the fields that I loved so much. I came here to cry unto God for help. And so I climbed, just as we are doing now."

I had never heard this part of the story. I looked toward the top of the hill. "Where are we going?"

My father answered by pointing to a pile of rocks located there. The expression on his face told me it held special significance. From the meadow below, as I tended the sheep, I had often noticed the rocks, but I had never considered it as anything more than another pile of rocks that were common to the area. Now my father's reverence for the pile seemed to suggest that it was something more—something sacred, like a monument or an altar. I was suddenly seized with the fear that my father was about to use this pile of rocks to preach to me, and for that I did not have time. I looked to the sun, rising toward the point of mid-morning, and then anxiously toward Jerusalem, searching my mind for a way to excuse myself.

Before I could speak, he continued with his story. "My pain was unbearable that day. My heart was broken, and I did not think it could be mended. But despite my agony, I could not deny that God loved me. I needed only to look into your face to see the evidence of that love. Somewhere in my suffocating grief, I knew that I had never been abandoned before and that God surely would not do so now in my darkest hour. So the question remained: *Would I abandon Him?*" Gesturing toward the pile of rocks, my father said, "And so I built it."

I did not understand.

My father took me by the arm, guiding me around the structure with evident admiration. He reverently placed his hand on the pile of rocks and said, "This is my Ebenezer."

Sudden understanding shot through me. In a distant moment of desperation, when our fathers had twice been defeated by the Philistines and had lost the ark of the covenant to their enemies, they had pleaded with God for help. Their vital prayer invoked the intervention of heaven and provided them courage. They rose up to fight again, defeated the Philistines, and took back the ark. To commemorate that victorious battle, the prophet Samuel set up a marker stone and named it *Ebenezer* or "Stone of Help."

With astonishment, I said to my father, "You built an Ebenezer?"

He nodded. "This is where God helped me that day. This place is where I cried my allegiance to Him: 'Nothing could cause me to forsake thee.' And it was on that day that I wrote my proverb of faith: 'God created today for us, to live and to love—in the safety of His fold, God will bless us today.'"

My father looked into my eyes. "Joshua, if the worst happens, will you cry your allegiance to God today?"

I slumped to my knees and began to weep. I could not answer honestly. If God were to take my wife from me, I did not know if I would understand. I did not know if I could continue to believe in such a being, one whom I had been taught was all-powerful and yet one who failed to save my sweet Miriam. I feared that I might forever accuse Him of abandoning us when we needed Him the most. I was ashamed that I did not possess my father's courage and faith. Through tears I answered, "I am not that brave."

My father knelt beside me, embraced me in his arms, and wept. "You *are* brave, Joshua," he said, "and I believe in you. I will pray that God helps you today."

When we descended the mount, I surveyed the rough Judean landscape and tried to take strength from it. This was the land of promise that God had given his chosen people. It was a harsh, unforgiving land that nevertheless had been envied and overrun by our enemies over the years, most recently by the Romans. And yet this land and its people had endured again and again by rallying around the covenants of our fathers. This land was the land of patriarchs and prophets, kings and priests of God. Over the centuries, the combined consciousness of nations had been riveted on this land.

As I gazed out over our flock of sheep, I felt a sense of resolve and realized that my father had given me what I had needed from him. Now standing a little taller, I said, "I know what I must do."

My father seemed to understand. He asked, "Which lamb will you choose for your offering?" But I supposed he already knew the answer. Nearly a year before, when I had been guarding the sheep, a jackal had leapt the wall of the sheepfold and charged a newborn lamb. Its mother had defended the lamb with her life. The entire event took only moments, but by the time I had rushed to rescue the pair, the ewe was dead. Thereafter, I took the lamb and raised it as my own. I gave it a name: *Amit*, meaning "friend."

As the lamb grew, he became as dear to me as if he were my child. I sheltered him, cared for him, and calmed him. Once, I thought I had lost him. He had fallen into a crevice at night. I called for him, but he did not respond. Resorting to another form of communication, I struck the ground three times with my staff, turned it upside down, made a cup of my hand, and cooed through it, my voice running along the staff and out to the lamb. I called for him in this manner all through the night before I heard his "baa, baa."

I left my flock with the other shepherds to find my lost lamb. I followed the sound of his bleating and found him, balanced precariously on a rock ledge deep in the crevice. Leaning over, I called down to him, "Don't be afraid, Amit. I am coming. Did you think you were lost? Did you think I had forgotten about you? I will always come for you."

After I had rescued Amit, I gathered him in my arms, kissed him, set him on my shoulders, and carried him home. When I returned to the fold, the other sheep came running to us. Oh, how they loved Amit. On that day, I cried out my gratitude to God for having helped me find my little lost lamb.

Feeling profound sorrow, I gazed at Amit now. I had not intended to raise him to be sacrificed on the altar of the temple. But now, knowing what was at stake, I felt I had no other choice. My father had taught me that true faith and worship require offering the best and most precious things to God. So, with a sense of purpose and yet with great sadness, I called Amit to me. When my little lamb bounded to me, bleating and happy, I lifted him into my arms, nuzzled him gently, and set him on my shoulders. I looked at my father with grief and yet with determination. He nodded. We understood each other. With that, he handed me a purse filled with a few coins and a scrip containing a little food. "For your journey," he said.

I thanked him and glanced back toward the high place where my father's Ebenezer stood. Then I turned my face toward Jerusalem.

Chapter 3

IN SEARCH OF A REDEEMER

Jerusalem lay northward—two Roman miles to Bethlehem then a climb of six more miles to the Holy City. Carrying a lamb on my shoulders was a burden, but nevertheless I pushed to quicken my gait. Time was a luxury I did not have.

Hooding my eyes with a hand, I looked skyward to check the position of the sun. I estimated that if I hurried I could arrive in Jerusalem by early afternoon and make my way to the temple shortly thereafter.

Amit was not cooperating. He bleated and struggled, obviously uncomfortable. He seemed irritated that his activities had been interrupted. I spoke reassuringly to him, but I knew his fate: Amit was destined to become my offering to God. Besides Miriam, Amit represented the best that I could give.

Certainly a merciful God would not hesitate to respond to such a sacrifice; surely He would hear and answer my pleading and save my wife. Imagining the rush of emotions that I would surely feel when the time came for me to offer my precious lamb on the altar of the temple, I tried to steel myself. Amit had become as dear to me as if he were my child.

As I hurried toward Bethlehem, I observed other shepherds leading their flocks to green pastures. They seemed completely unaware of my presence or plight. I wondered how an event as urgent as mine could go unnoticed. The shepherds were conducting their sheep along winding paths to fertile hillsides with nearby brooks.

I thought about my father and our fellow shepherds of Beit Sahour. To a passerby we might have seemed indistinguishable from other shepherds—ordinary, except for the extraordinary sheep that comprised our flock. Our sheep had been culled from other flocks and consecrated to a holy purpose. The yearlings shared a common destiny; they would be offered on the great altar at the temple in Jerusalem to fulfill the Mosaic law of sacrifice. Consequently, we who kept these sheep were specifically trained for this royal task.

The closer I came to Bethlehem the more congested the road became. I passed a young family. The man was leading a donkey with a little boy perched on its back, and his wife was herding two other small children, who were as cooperative as kittens. The woman seemed exhausted from the effort, her stomach showing evidence of another child on the way. The man called out to me, "Are you going to Bethlehem?"

"Yes," I replied, "and from thence to Jerusalem."

"For Passover, I presume." He indicated the lamb on my shoulders. The celebration of Passover was fast approaching, and over two million people would soon converge on Jerusalem.

"No," I answered, "I am going to the temple, and then I will return home."

The man seemed intrigued by my answer. "Do you live nearby?"

"In Beit Sahour," I replied, becoming anxious now. The conversation had slowed me, and I had not the time to pause and talk.

"We are from Cana," he said. "We are going to Bethlehem for the taxing." He made this last statement with a tone of disgust. Recently Caesar had ordered a census of his empire, accompanied by a taxing. Caesar's edict had provided our Jewish leaders an opportunity to count the populace of Israel according to ancestry. Therefore, each family head was to return to his ancestral town to fulfill both the Roman and the Jewish proclamations. The man continued, "Do you know of an inn in Bethlehem?"

"There are several," I replied. "Chinham's khan is the

oldest and best known." When I had said so, I looked at his pregnant wife and considered her discomfort in such a place. Even for the most hardened travelers, a khan was a hard place to sleep.

Chinham's khan was no exception. Miriam and I had once lodged in the seven-hundred-year-old inn. It was a large, bare building, constructed of rough stones boasting two levels of guestrooms, which were mere recesses cut in the walls. These rooms had no fronts and offered no privacy. Because everything that took place in a guestroom was visible to any guest in the khan, I had draped a blanket over the opening to allow my wife her modesty.

I asked the man if he had brought blankets to sleep on. The stone floors would be cold this time of year.

"Yes," he replied. "We would not consider a khan if our family in Bethlehem had room for us. But with the taxing and Passover . . ."

I nodded that I understood, wished him well, and began to pick up my pace. The man was not finished. He called after me, "Is there a place to stable my donkey in the khan?"

I answered him, "Yes, of course. There is a central open-air courtyard below the room, where you can tie up your donkey." Then considering his wife and small children, I added, "But you really must hurry to Bethlehem.

The rooms are sure to fill up before nightfall, and then you will have no choice except to make do in the lower courtyard among the animals."

The thought of clearing out an unoccupied corner of the stable to make a place to sleep made me feel ill. The stables of khans were perpetually filthy and crowded with sheep, horses, cattle, mules, and camels. The stench would be overwhelming, and achieving sleep in such a place would prove challenging.

Suddenly, the donkey stumbled and shied, and the boy riding on its back slipped off, landing on his shoulder. The child screamed in pain and in fright, and his parents ran to him. I took the rope tied to the donkey to hold him steady. The mother hovered over the yelping boy, and the father said, "Is his shoulder broken?"

"I don't know," the mother said. The other children were crying now. The donkey brayed, and Amit bleated wildly.

I set Amit on the ground and held him close in one hand while clinging to the rope in the other. "Will you allow me to examine the boy?" I asked.

"Do you know of such things?" said the mother.

"I am a shepherd and often deal with breaks and bruises."

The parents stepped aside. The mother gathered her

little ones to her, and the father took the rope to the donkey. Amit remained close by me as I knelt beside the wailing boy and gently felt for breaks. "Do not cry," I said. "I will not hurt you."

I spoke to him as I would have talked to my sheep, with quiet reassurance. Soon the child settled down, and I felt the bones in his shoulder and sternum for breaks. The boy allowed me to work with him, and at length, finding no permanent damage, I took him in my arms, and he wrapped his arms around my neck and laid his head on my shoulder. As I rubbed his back, I imagined doing this for my own son—an experience I might never have. Then his mother reached out her arms, and the boy quickly went to her. I said, "He's fine. Just a little scared."

The mother smiled. "You must be a father."

I shook my head. "Not yet."

"Then you are married?" she asked. When I nodded, she said, "Your wife is very fortunate."

"I am the fortunate one," I said. With that I gathered Amit into my arms and set him again upon my shoulders.

The man said, "My wife and I have been married for six years, and you can see the harvest." He laughed and indicated the three children and the one on its way. Then he asked, "Have you been married long?"

"Seven years," I replied.

His expression became one of embarrassment. His wife began to apologize for him. "We didn't mean to pry."

"You could not have known," I said. "But I really must be going . . ."

With apparent understanding, the man said, "You are going to the temple to pray, aren't you?" He indicated the lamb on my shoulders. I nodded. He paused a moment and said, "By the way you treat this lamb, it must be very special." I nodded again. Then his eyes grew wide. "You are going to pray for your wife."

My eyes filled with tears, and I could not answer. The man's wife stepped forward as if to comfort me. "We have kept you too long. You have been so kind to us. What can we do for you?"

I turned my head, causing the young children to ask why this stranger was crying. The mother knelt to quiet them, and the man put a hand on my shoulder and said, "We will pray for you."

I thanked him. "I must cross through Bethlehem in haste. I must hurry to the temple and then back to my wife."

The man blessed me by the God of Israel and said, "Go in peace."

I entered Bethlehem breathing hard. I had not made as much progress as I had hoped, and that reality tortured me. My temple errand grew more urgent with every passing moment. I must hurry through town and on to Jerusalem. I would only stop briefly to drink at the well.

As I hurried along the streets of Bethlehem, I was struck by the congestion in this little place. Bethlehem and neighboring Ephrathah were small villages, boasting fewer than five hundred residents combined. But now Bethlehem's narrow streets seemed as crowded as Jerusalem's great Hippodrome on the day of chariot races.

Adding to the confusion were the animals that accompanied the visitors. My senses were assaulted by the noise and odor of myriad sheep, cattle, camels, and donkeys.

The scene was a mass of confusion—each animal being driven by its master to an undefined location; every family seeking accommodations; each father pressing toward a publican—a tax collector—to submit to the taxation and begrudgingly hand over money that few could spare.

To the chorus of bleating, bellowing, and braying, Amit added his cry and his legs began to flail. I held him more securely and moved on toward the center of town and its well of spring water.

Bethlehem, I judged, was anything but peaceful. I had relatives here, but if I had expected to see them—and I had not—my expectation would have been in error. I could never have found them in this ocean of humanity.

I agreed with the man I had met on the road: such crowdedness and disorder could only be the work of Romans. The great Octavian—Caesar Augustus—had once again flexed his muscle, and because the Emperor was supreme, the world had cowered at his command. Even God's chosen people. We, too, must bow again under the rod of Rome and be obliged to live in silent contempt of our conqueror or suffer our hatred to be nailed with us to the cross.

We had little recourse from the oppression of Rome, and we received no relief from our king, Herod the Great, Rome's puppet, who ruled Judea with a bloody hand. Considering the myriads of poor, downtrodden people before me now, I wondered if the world had ever known tyrants as ruthless as Caesar and Herod. These cutthroats and the troops at their disposal, stationed in Jerusalem and elsewhere, were a constant reminder of our bondage.

As I surveyed Bethlehem, its poor and oppressed once again suffering under the edicts of Caesar and Herod, I longed for the promised Messiah, the Son of David, to deliver us, as had been promised by the prophets. The rabbis taught that this great deliverer would redeem Israel and return her to her ancient glory. Now, standing in Bethlehem, the birthplace of David, all I could do was mourn. Where was David's son? We needed him now. As I watched the people file through the narrow streets toward Caesar's and Herod's corrupt tax collectors, I despaired at our nation's hope for a redeemer.

Interrupting my thoughts, the shriek of a woman pierced through me. I spun around to see a young woman fighting off two Roman soldiers, one of whom was trying to shackle her and the other to rip her baby from her arms. The child was screaming.

Instinctively, I moved toward her. The incident had drawn a crowd of onlookers, some sympathetic and others curious. No one offered to help. I stretched to see the woman. Adjacent to me stood an aged man and woman who spoke to each other as though they understood what was happening.

I asked the man, "What has the woman done?"

The old woman answered for him. "The publican has condemned her because she cannot pay the tax." The old woman's mouth was vacant except for several bottom teeth. She was short and round, and I had to bend low to hear her.

The young woman continued to cry out as the soldier wrestled her child from her and the other pinned her arms behind her back. The terrified child wailed. The crowd uttered a collective gasp. We knew that none of us was exempt from such treatment; each of us could imagine ourselves in the woman's situation. Living under the tyranny of Rome, we were always one misstep away from harsh retribution. "Can no one help her?" I asked. "Where is her family?"

"Her husband is dead," the old woman replied.

"Then you know her?" I asked.

"Yes. She is from Ephrathah. When her husband died, he left her destitute and with a child. His brother agreed to marry her, but then he broke the marriage contract. Now she has no *go'el*. The Romans will flog her, and then she will be forced into slavery to pay the tax. Her child will be sold."

I understood the gravity of the old woman's words. Without a *go'el*, the young woman's future was bleak indeed. God had made provision for the widows in Israel.

When a husband died, his brother or a kinsman was to marry the deceased man's wife to give her security. That man became her *go'el,* meaning "redeemer." As I considered the woman's plight, I knew that a second marriage would have freed her from debt and elevated her esteem among the people. But because her brother-in-law had abandoned her, she would become an outcast of Israel and a criminal of Rome.

The young woman cried out again, but this time it was with despairing resignation. Suddenly, she went limp. Her expression was that of a fawn, who having been shot through, looks at his own fur on the arrow that kills him. I pushed through the crowd and hurried toward her. The soldier holding her shrieking baby reached for his sword. I stopped short and put up a hand as if it were a shield. "I mean no harm," I shouted, knowing that defying Rome could end in crucifixion.

"Do you know this woman?" the soldier asked.

"Yes," I lied. The woman looked at me with a bewildered expression. I made a gesture, hoping to signal her to follow my lead.

Cautiously, I stepped near her, the soldier tightening his grip on the handle of his sword. But when he made no further movement to prevent me, I turned and looked upon the woman, searching my mind for a way to help her.

I judged her to be about Miriam's age, remarkably beautiful, dark-eyed, skin the color of goat's milk. She was a wisp of a girl, frightened, vulnerable, and as delicate as a lily petal, certainly no match for the publican or the soldiers. I gazed at her with pity, and then suddenly I heard myself announce, "She is my . . . *sister*."

A low murmur swept through the crowd. The woman's eyes spoke confusion and then reflected a glimmer of hope. I tried to hold my expression firm so as not to betray my lie, praying that the officials would not ask me her name. The soldier holding the woman jerked her arm hard and asked her, "Is it true? Is he your brother?" When she hesitated, he jerked again.

"Yes," she whimpered.

"What has she done to deserve this treatment?" I demanded. Romans only responded to the language of force. I took a bold step toward the soldier holding her. His eyes darted nervously between the crowd and me, as if he were a rat caught between two cats.

Apparently sensing the tension, the publican stood up from behind his table and said, "She refuses to pay the tax."

"That's not true!" the woman cried. "I have no money to pay it, and I have nothing to sell."

The soldier holding the woman spun her around and backhanded her across the mouth, sending her sprawling. I rushed to her and pushed aside the soldier. He drew his sword and brandished it at me. The crowd took a step back. I held Amit in one arm as my only defense. When I put up the other to wave off the soldier, I called out to the publican, "How much is her assessment?"

"Twenty silver shekels for the woman, plus ten for the child."

Thirty shekels—the price of a slave! In my entire life, I had never had that much money at one time. I glanced at the woman and locked eyes with her, both of us seeking a solution that eluded us. I considered the purse of coins that my father had given me for my journey, but I knew it contained only a few mites, enough for a little food but no more.

And then I knew what I must do. The thought crushed me with sadness. I also knew that Miriam, had she been present, would insist on this solution. I knew I could never live with myself if I did not act, as I felt prompted to at this moment. Sadly, I gazed at Amit. Then turning to the publican, I asked, "Will you accept my lamb for the debt?" I yelled the question loudly, so that my offer rang in the ears of the onlookers. I knew that a lamb could never be worth the price of the woman's debt, but I was counting on public pressure to negotiate a settlement.

The publican was a short bull of a man, stout of build, heavily bearded, with black expressionless eyes. His fine clothing betrayed his success as a tax collector, who was allowed to keep part of each assessment. The publican put a hand to his chin as if to ponder my offer. His delay prompted a low, angry murmur from the crowd that encircled us. He lowered his hand and surveyed the people, realizing that the situation might grow out of control. Then he glanced nervously at the soldiers, who had also taken note of the unrest. He frowned and then turned to me and nodded. With that, he motioned for a soldier to fetch my lamb.

I was not prepared to lose Amit so abruptly. The soldier severed my lamb from me, and I felt a sensation not unlike running a thumb along the edge of a blade. Amit bleated wildly. I reached out for him, but the soldier was swift, and in a sudden movement, he spirited Amit away. I staggered under the weight of the loss. Now, watching him disappear into the crowd in the soldier's arms, my mind flooded with memories.

I had taken Amit to myself when he was orphaned, at a particularly low point in my life, when Miriam and I imagined that she would never conceive again. Amit became the child I thought I would never have. I lavished upon him my affection. I fed him, loved him, and gave him a name. He was beautiful, as perfect and spotless a lamb as I had ever seen. When I called to him, he would bound toward me, bleating happily. I would play with him, sing to him, and stroke him every night when I bedded him down, as though he were my child. He always pastured nearby. I grieved, knowing that tonight Amit would be the publican's supper.

The other soldier stepped toward the woman and roughly handed her the baby. She buried her face in the bundle and wept. Reunited with its mother, the child sobbed at first and then whimpered. The onlookers became silent, as if they had just entered a sanctuary. I looked at the people to encourage them to step forward and offer the woman comfort. But perhaps because they feared the Romans, they withheld their compassion. I was profoundly disappointed. My occupation as a shepherd had taught me that a lost or wounded sheep needed the comfort of others in order to heal. Because the curious people would not help her, I motioned for them to disperse. One by one they departed.

Alone now, I knelt beside the young woman. She reminded me of a frightened lamb that had been separated from the flock. With the instinct of a shepherd, I reached out a comforting hand to touch her on the shoulder, but she did not immediately respond. I understood.

When a sheep was sick or hurt, a shepherd would need to exercise empathy and patience. He would run his hand over the sheep's head and down its back until he found a spot where the sheep could feel a connection. Then when the sheep responded to the touch, the shepherd could begin the healing process.

This woman needed the calming hand of a shepherd. Tenderly, I reached out and touched her hand. She did not withdraw it. Her breathing became more measured, and she looked up at me gratefully. I pulled back the covering from her baby and gazed at him. I smiled and asked, "What is your child's name?"

The young woman dried her eyes and answered proudly, "Gideon."

"And yours?" I asked.

"Rebekah." She paused. "Thank you," she said softly. "Thank you for both of us."

I nodded. "I, too, have a wife and a—" I was about to say "child," but I caught myself.

"They must be so fortunate," she said. "My husband was much like you. Kind, generous . . ." Her eyes filled with tears.

Embarrassed, I turned my head and waited for her to compose herself. Finally, I asked, "How long has he been gone?"

"Six months tomorrow."

"You have no one?"

She looked at her child and began to cry again. "My husband has a brother—" She could not continue.

"I understand," I said, touching her hand again. "Is there no one else?"

"My parents are dead. I have no brothers or sisters, but I have relatives in Capernaum."

"Could you go to them?"

She pondered my question and then offered a slight nod.

"Then you must go to them immediately," I said. "Do you have any money to make the journey?"

She cried and shook her head. I thought for a moment and then removed the cloak from my shoulders. "This is made of fine wool," I said. "It will fetch a good price. Take it and sell it for your journey."

Rebekah resisted. "No, you mustn't. You have already done so much, and you don't even know me."

I gazed down at her son then at her, and smiled kindly. "I know you," I said. "You are my sister."

She buried her head in my shoulder and wept. She answered softly, "And you are my *go'el*. This day you have redeemed us."

I departed Bethlehem empty-handed and cold, but strangely my heart felt full and warm. As much as I could, I avoided thinking about Amit; so many emotions were crushing me already. Instead I gathered my energy to focus on Miriam and the quest before me. I must still go up to Jerusalem and in the temple petition God for her life.

My mind filled with uncertainty. Without a lamb, I did not know how I would make an offering. I had been taught that a prayer without a sacrifice is only half a prayer. I reached for the purse that my father had given me and counted five mites, coins of slender value. I allowed myself the luxury of unrealistic optimism: maybe I could use the money to barter for another lamb in the temple courtyard. But reason prevailed, and I discarded the notion. Such a small amount could not purchase another lamb.

As I left the northern entrance of Bethlehem, I entered the Hebron Road that led to Jerusalem. Marking that spot was the tomb of Rachel, Jacob's beloved wife.

She had died giving birth to her son Benjamin while she and Jacob were traveling from Bethel to Hebron. A monument had been erected there to her memory. I was a Benjamite and proud to be one of her descendants.

As I passed by Rachel's memorial, I thought of her courage and the sacrifice that she had made to bring a child of promise into the world. Then I thought about Rebekah and Gideon. They would be on their way to Capernaum to be with family, freed by the price of a lamb.

And I thought about Miriam and the child I would never know.

Chapter 4

JERUSALEM—
THE ETERNAL CITY

I approached Jerusalem on the Hebron Road as I climbed up out of the Hinnom Valley. The prophets had compared this place to hell. The valley formed a deep, narrow ravine at the foot of the walls of the city, where Jerusalem's refuse was burned. Because the refuse eternally burned, it had provided an object lesson for prophets, whose burden it was to warn Israel of the consequences of wickedness and to purify her to receive her king, the promised Messiah.

This place was also where the bodies of executed criminals and other infamous people were dumped. I observed such a scene now. Several Roman soldiers had driven a cart to the outskirts of the city, followed by a group of wailing women. As the soldiers hefted a body from the cart and tossed it into the smoldering refuse pile, one of the women collapsed and the others knelt beside her in an effort to console her.

I could only imagine that the deceased was related to her, and because Romans were involved, the dead person

47

had probably suffered crucifixion. The body would never be honored by being washed, anointed with spices, and wrapped in burial linen. It was simply another carcass to be discarded. I turned my head from this scene of death. I had been haunted by too much of it today.

Since the time that I had left Bethlehem, I had passed several bands of pilgrims going up to Jerusalem to celebrate the approaching Passover. I moved more quickly now that I was no longer carrying a lamb. Each group greeted me as I neared, but I didn't slow or linger. In each woman's face, I saw Miriam; in each child, I was reminded of the son I would never know. I returned their greetings but did not slow to share their joy or sing with them the traditional Psalms of Ascent.

As I passed them, I heard them sing of deliverance, redemption, and the hope of a Messiah. I heard fathers rehearse to their children the meaning of Passover, when the angel of death passed over the homes of our fathers, killed the firstborn of the Egyptians, and set Israel free. Although I listened to their exultations, I did not feel to rejoice. My heart was too heavy and my anxiety too high. I simply prayed that the angel of death would once again pass over us and deliver my Miriam today.

The number of pilgrims going up to Jerusalem impressed me. They were many, but I knew from experience that their numbers were relatively small compared to the hundreds of thousands who would shortly press into Jerusalem for Passover. But celebrating deliverance was not my purpose today; to petition God for deliverance was.

When I climbed out of the Hinnom Valley, I beheld Jerusalem, the Eternal City, rising breathtakingly like an ensign in the golden sun. To Israel, Jerusalem was the most sacred place on earth, traditionally the center place where God had first set down his foot on the morn of creation. Leaving Hinnom Valley and approaching Jerusalem, I felt as though I were climbing out of hell and was about to enter heaven. As I viewed the gates of the holy city, my hope surged. Surely God was here. I only prayed that he would help me today.

I entered Jerusalem through Zion's Gate, passing under the arch of the imposing wall that surrounded the city. I entered the lower city, where the poorer people lived. The small houses here were built hard up against each other. Narrow, earthen streets ran every which way, causing visitors to become easily lost. Most of the streets and alleys were unpaved, a combination of pounded earth and stone. I asked a man for directions to the temple. He pointed off to an obscure point on the horizon and rattled off instructions I did not fully understand. Before I reached the temple, I would need to ask directions twice more.

I quickened my step. Now that I had entered Jerusalem, the thought of my prayer for Miriam was acutely on my mind, more than it had been all day. That I must hurry to the temple to pray was my single objective. I looked up in the direction of the sun and noted that it was beginning to dip toward the western horizon. I hoped I was not too late. When I reached the temple, I would need to procure an animal somehow for my offering. A lamb would be best, but a turtledove would be acceptable. When I remembered losing Amit, I felt as though a deep wound had reopened; the hurt was still fresh. I reached for the purse strapped to my tunic and considered again the improbability of purchasing another lamb with the few coins that it held. Perhaps someone might take pity on me. I quickly discarded that fantasy. No, a turtledove would have to do.

Not knowing Miriam's present condition added to my distress. Picturing her lying in her soiled bed, agonizing with each contraction, with the worried women gathered around, I struggled to hold onto hope. Tears began to form in my eyes again. They were coming more easily now. I felt ashamed and looked around, hoping that no one had noticed. It was unmanly to appear so emotional, but I was incapable of holding back.

At the edge of the lower city, just as I was to break free of it, I came upon a scene that caused me to slow momentarily. Before me stood a marriage canopy, and within the adjoining house I heard the sounds of celebration. A new family had been added to Israel.

My mind was suddenly overwhelmed with memories of Miriam. On the occasion of Miriam's and my wedding, seven years before, my relatives had likewise gathered to celebrate our nuptials. It was unforgettable. Miriam's mother, Leah, had seen to that.

Like all Jewish children, Miriam and I had been taught that we were born to marry. As teenagers, we became officially betrothed, promised to each other before our families and other witnesses. Neither of us had been surprised at the occasion of our betrothal. It had been planned and negotiated between our parents years before it took place.

Tradition called for me to offer Miriam's father a bride-price for his daughter. Because I was very poor, I had managed to save only twenty denarii, a paltry amount, considering it was supposed to represent my bride's value. I wanted to offer more. I wanted to show Miriam that her worth to me could not be measured by money. Therefore, I increased the bride-price by offering to work for two years for Miriam's father in the same way that my forefather Jacob had worked for his father-in-law to win Rachel. Thereafter, I prepared a marriage contract, wherein I pledged to provide and care for Miriam with all my heart, might, mind, and soul. I was overjoyed when Miriam and her father accepted all the terms, including my meager bride-price offering.

The thought of caring for Miriam tortured me now. Did my leaving her today constitute an act of caring or an act of desperation? She had asked me to go, to offer up a sacrifice and ask God to bless us, but had I been wise to leave her? When I finally offered my prayer in the temple to plead for God's intervention, would my faith be strong enough to summon the Sovereign of the Universe to condescend to save her? Would God indeed bless us today?

Still thinking of the newly married couple, I recalled the fond details of our betrothal. On that occasion, when Miriam's father accepted the bride-price and I had offered Miriam the marriage contract, one more step remained: Miriam must drink the cup of acceptance. Because she could not be forced to become betrothed, she must drink from the cup to signify her acceptance of my offer. This was a moment of trepidation. I poured wine into a cup and handed it to Miriam. My father, her parents, the friend of the bridegroom, and two witnesses surrounded us. Despite my having known for years that this day was coming, I began to tremble when Miriam took the cup in her right hand. I prayed that she would accept me. When she finally drank it, I wept for joy.

This woman would be my wife, I thought, a virgin most fair and beautiful, the gemstone of Beit Sahour, a maiden without an equal. How I had come to win her heart I could not divine. At that point, Miriam's father stepped forward and blessed us. As a final gesture, I handed Miriam a coin, the traditional betrothal gift of love. As I placed the coin in her hand, I repeated the words, "By this, thou art set apart for me according to the laws of Moses and of Israel." Now we were betrothed to be married.

The most difficult part of our betrothal was holding to tradition and taking my leave. I would not see my beloved for nearly two years while I constructed the wedding chamber, which would become our home. The thought of leaving my beloved Miriam tortured me. I hated being away from her. Even now, after seven years of marriage, when she was out of my sight for very long, I would find myself gazing at the sun to estimate the time when I could be with her again.

I thought about the couple that had just married: they had no idea what life had in store for them. Over the ensuing years would they, too, lose three children before they were born? Seven years from now, would the wife be fighting for her life while her husband rushed to the temple to pray for her? Would their love for each other and their faith in God prove sufficient to weather life's storms and guide them through their wilderness to their promised land?

Through the two years of our betrothal, I was true to my vow. I worked for Miriam's father while I built a room in my father's house for my bride. The wait, of course, was agony. I survived it by remaining busy. I constructed the wedding chamber under my father's supervision, and he did not allow me to shirk. "You are making this chamber for Miriam," he would remind me, as though he loved her more than I. His insistence on quality protracted the time, and because I needed his permission to claim my wife, I was obligated to make improvements until he was satisfied.

One day he approached me while I was provisioning the interior and examined my work. I steeled myself for another round of suggestions. But this time, he walked the circumference without saying a word. Then he turned and said, "You are finished. Go receive your bride." My long wait had finally ended. At last, Miriam would be mine.

Miriam did not know the hour of my coming. That uncertainty required her to live in a constant state of preparation and watchfulness, ever anticipating the time when I might come for her. Every bridegroom chooses a friend to help him through the process of betrothal and oversee the marriage. My friend was my cousin Aaron. During the betrothal he had shuttled back and forth between Miriam and me, conveying messages.

"Have you seen her today?" I would ask him.

Aaron loved to tease. Often, he would say yes then begin to walk away.

"Wait!" I would beg him. "What does she look like?" Sometimes I had to resort to wrestling to pry the details from him.

"She is beautiful," he would say.

"Then you have seen her."

"Yes. She wears a veil in public with a chain of ten pieces of silver."

That pleased me, of course. As a betrothed woman, Miriam wore a veil with the chain of coins hiding her face to signify that she was spoken for—she was mine. I would ask Aaron, "What does she say? Does she have a message for me?" Aaron's face would turn red. "What is it?" I would demand.

"Something about . . . she loves you," he would reply.

My heart would race. I would press for more details. "Is she preparing for my coming?"

"Yes. She has purified herself, and virgins attend her day and night." Aaron's statement held high significance for me. That Miriam was preparing herself through ritual immersion meant that she was symbolically turning away from her former life and readying herself to start a new life with me. The virgins who attended her were Miriam's bridesmaids. They lived in an attitude of readiness, keeping oil in their lamps for the night that I would come for my bride. These customs were steeped in tradition, of course, and delighted every bride.

My father had given his permission, so I spent the remainder of the day preparing to go to claim my bride. I dressed in borrowed finery, jewelry, and a crown—as if I were a king. Marriage represented a coronation.

As midnight approached, my family and friends formed a procession and started out for Miriam's home. Our lamps illumined the dark streets of Beit Sahour like the harvest moon, and we paraded through the streets to the sounds of music and tambourines. The entire town awakened at the sounds of my coming. Messengers preceded me. They trumpeted and shouted, *"Behold, the bridegroom! Come out to meet him."*

When I arrived at Miriam's home, I found her waiting for me, dressed in regal attire and anointed with sweet-smelling oil. Her hair was braided with precious stones, and she wore beautiful jewelry befitting a queen. I conveyed her from her home, and in a flood of lamplight, the wedding assembly moved off in a festal procession of song and dance to the place that I had prepared for her.

When we arrived at our new home, we stepped under the canopy and faced each other. Then the rabbi pronounced blessings upon us. He fastened our hands together with an ornate ribbon and gave us a cup of wine that we drank to seal the marriage covenant. At last, Miriam and I were married.

I took one last look at the marriage canopy of this newly married couple and moved on toward the temple, silently offering them my congratulations. I doubted that the husband, or any husband, could love his bride as I much as I loved Miriam, but even if his love amounted to a fraction of mine, he would be a fortunate man indeed.

I broke from my recollections as I emerged from the narrow streets of the lower city and beheld the Temple Mount. I doubted that anything so grand existed anywhere in the world. At the center of the Temple Mount stood the holy temple—the house of the Lord, the sacred structure that connected earth and heaven. The temple dwarfed all other structures in the complex. The common saying rang true: "He who has not seen the temple has not seen anything beautiful." I started across the long bridge that led to the gates of the temple, surveying as I went the massive retaining walls that supported and surrounded the Temple Mount.

I looked up at the imposing pinnacle of the temple. There, every morning, a priest would sound his trumpet to signal the beginning of the daily sacrifices. I imagined standing atop the pinnacle and taking in the spectacular view. From there, I could have seen all Jerusalem, the Romans' Antonia Fortress at the corner of Temple Mount, Herod's opulent palace near the city walls, and beyond the walls, I would have seen the ominous Golgotha, the frightening rocky hill with cavities that resembled the eyes of a skull. Opposite Golgotha, I would have seen the Mount of Olives with its beautiful garden called Gethsemane.

I arrived at a wide set of steps that led into the Temple Mount. At the top of these steps stood the Huldah Gates, and before the gates were three pools. Dozens of people were congregated here, waiting to ritually purify themselves in the pools in order to gain access to the most sacred precincts of the temple. I felt the need to remain polite as I anxiously waited my turn, but the day was waning, as was my patience.

A young woman with long, flowing brown hair stood with her back to me. A thought shot through my mind that she was Miriam, and instinct nudged me to reach for her. But I caught myself when she turned. She smiled at me, and I returned it awkwardly. Miriam was so much on my mind now that I found myself searching for her in every young woman's face. After I had purified myself, I hurried to enter through the temple gates. I could no longer afford delays. Beggars and the infirm called out to me, but I looked past them as I hurried on.

I came to a long, dim staircase that ran under the Temple Mount and emerged in the court of the temple above. I took the stairs in quick strides and soon stepped out of the darkness into the brightness of light. I had the feeling that I had entered a celestial world, and I felt hope surge within me. I was now standing in the huge Court of the Gentiles, so named because anyone of any nationality or religion was allowed here. My eyes and ears told me that there were indeed many nationalities in this place. I observed renowned rabbis teaching their disciples at various locations in the courtyard. I also noticed more blind and crippled people begging throughout the court—so many that one could easily become numb to their plight. Once again, I chose to ignore them, and I hurried on.

I spotted a Levite, dressed in his white temple robes and tubular hat, directing worshippers and advising them what kind of sacrifices were to be performed. I approached him and asked, "Where might I purchase a turtledove?"

He swept his hand across the Court of the Gentiles and said, "Take your pick." I was embarrassed that in my rush I had not paid sufficient attention. The Court of the Gentiles was filled with vendors selling sacrificial animals, souvenirs, and food. He looked at me suspiciously and asked, "Do you have money?"

"A little," I answered. Then touching the scrip that hung from my belt, "I have but five mites."

The Levite frowned. "Where are you from?"

"Beit Sahour," I answered impatiently. "Do you think I might purchase a turtledove for five mites?"

"Beit Sahour," he mused. Then with sudden understanding, he said, "So you are a shepherd."

He said it with a tone of disdain. Shepherds were considered the lowest of society. We had no standing in the courts of the law and were not even allowed to testify there. That I had entered the temple at all was taking a risk. "It is true that I am a shepherd," I answered boldly. "My flock supplies many sacrificial lambs for the temple."

The Levite seemed to size up my statement but appeared impressed. "Then you are one of the shepherds under special rabbinical instruction," he said. "You have been specifically trained for this royal task."

I was not willing to engage him in conversation. "Please, sir," I insisted, "I am in need of a turtledove."

"Of course," he answered. "There is a vendor at the door of the *Soreg*. He is known to be reasonable." With that, the Levite pointed me toward the entrance of the sacred inner temple court, where stood the temple proper.

I thanked him and made my way to the magnificent temple, rising breathtakingly heavenward above its high, imposing outer walls.

The temple's white, rose-accented limestone finish was so brilliant I had to shield my eyes to behold it. From a distance, the temple appeared like a great snow-clad mountain. Even in my haste I couldn't help but be in awe of the temple's construction. Parts of the structure were decorated with pure gold and precious blue and green gems. The gold and cool colors contrasted elegantly with the temple's dominant white exterior. Towering gold-plated pilasters added to the temple's beauty. Atop the pilasters were crenellations that lined the roof, suggesting the crown of a king. Taken in total, the temple provided a spectacular visual feast.

I hurried toward the inner temple compound to locate the vendor. In spite of my personal disdain for commerce in the temple area, I needed to purchase a turtledove to make an offering in conjunction with my prayer before rushing back to my Miriam.

When I came to the Beautiful Gate, the entrance leading into the temple's inner courts, I looked for the vendor but noticed a father and mother with their infant instead. The way that the child was wrapped suggested that it was a boy. The couple was young—much like Miriam and I in our first year of marriage. The mother wore a pale yellow tunic, the color of parchment. Her dark hair emerged from the sheer veil she wore on her head and flowed down to the middle of her back in soft waves. She reminded me so much of Miriam that I stopped and stared at her for a moment. She was lovingly cradling her baby while her husband asked questions and directions of temple-goers. This was apparently the first time that he and his wife had come to the temple, at least with a baby.

As I watched them, I began to mourn for the loss of my child. Had it been a boy, Miriam and I would have likewise brought him to the temple forty days after his birth to present him to the Lord and participate in the same sacred rites. We would have performed the ritual of redeeming our firstborn son by paying five shekels at the sanctuary. I imagined that this family had come to the temple today for that reason. Watching this young couple with their child, I felt a profound sense of loss. If today's events had been different, Miriam and I would have been standing here forty days from now, participating in these sacred rites.

An old man drew near to help the confused husband. After a short conversation, the old man motioned toward the Beautiful Gate, and the young husband smiled as if to thank him. At that point, the old man sought permission from the mother to hold the child. She obliged and handed him the bundle. Gathering the child into his arms, the old man gazed at the baby for a moment and then smiled politely and handed the child back to his mother. I thought I perceived disappointment in his face.

Regardless, the couple thanked him again before mounting the steps that led to the inner courts of the temple.

Sensing that the old man knew the precinct well, I stepped toward him and said, "Please excuse me. I couldn't help but notice your kindness. Do you know where I might purchase a turtledove? I was told there was a vendor here."

The old man seemed startled. He peered at me as if with recognition. "Do we know each other?" he asked.

I stared at him for a hint of familiarity. "No. I don't think so. I am just a visitor . . . from Beit Sahour."

"You're a shepherd," the old man observed. I expected another wave of condemnation, but I perceived that the old man was pleased he had guessed my profession.

"Yes, I am a shepherd," I replied.

I began to repeat my question when he said, "I know of your order and your service." Then gazing at me with real intent, he asked, "At night, while tending your flock, have you looked heavenward toward the east and watched for the coming of the new star?"

I shook my head. "What star?"

"It will be a new one—the star of Jacob, which shall herald the Messiah's birth."

I was startled that his pronouncement sounded imminent. Centuries earlier Moses had prophesied of such a star. I regarded the old man with mild disbelief. Here was another delusional fanatic, I thought. I was suddenly sorry that I had taken the occasion to talk to him. I hadn't the time. Making a movement to leave, I answered, "I am not a student of the heavens . . . and I have had other things on my mind lately." I began to excuse myself. "I really must be going. My wife has been with child, and I must—"

In a sudden burst of understanding, the old man interjected, "Your wife is with child?" He looked in the direction of Beautiful Gate and added, "Like the couple that just entered the Court of the Women?" His question had the tone of yearning, as if a long-sought hope depended upon my response. When I did not immediately answer, he grew serious, as if his mind were working on an idea. He studied my face; his eyes penetrated me. He reminded me of my father, who would gaze at me with that same searching look before saying something wise. Finally, the old man said, "You say you're from Beit Sahour. That is near Bethlehem." He paused. "And you say your wife is with child?"

I was growing uneasy. His examination evoked tender emotions in me. I dropped my eyes and replied softly, "The child has died in my wife's womb." I drew in a deep breath and added, "And now her life—" I could not continue.

The old man placed a hand on my shoulder and said, "I am sorry for prying. I perceive that you have come to the temple to pray for her today." I nodded. He offered a slight bow and said, "My name is Simeon. I come to the temple often. In a distant time, the Lord spoke peace to my heart and told me that I would live to see his salvation, the promised Messiah, before I died. One day I will find him here. When my eyes have beheld him, I will depart this life in peace. I will know for myself that salvation will come to all nations and glory will return to Israel." Simeon gazed at me again. He said, "The Child's father would be about your age—"

"I am not the man you seek," I replied abruptly. "My name is Joshua ben Levi. I have no child . . . but my wife may be dying. My only purpose in coming to the temple today is to pray for her."

"You have come seeking a miracle." Simeon's declaration was a statement of fact. After he had said it, he became suddenly firm, as if understanding had illuminated him. He squared himself before me and spoke with an authoritative voice, as if with the tongue of an angel. "God will bless you today, Joshua ben Levi."

Simeon's words penetrated me to the heart. I felt a shock shoot through my body as if I had been struck by lightning. Once again I felt as though Simeon could have been my father speaking. For a moment I could not utter a response. I felt weak. I took his hand, squeezed it hard, and whispered, "Thank you."

Still facing me, Simeon urged, "You must believe, Joshua. Even if life takes from you that which is most precious, you must hold true to your God and wait for his salvation." Then, motioning toward an old woman, who was ministering to a crippled man sitting at the entrance of the Beautiful Gate, he added, "There are others who believe and wait for the consolation of Israel. The woman's name is Anna. She married at fourteen and her husband died seven years later. For the last sixty-three years, she has been a widow. She spends her days in the temple fasting, praying, administering relief to God's children . . . and waiting for the Messiah."

I stared in disbelief at the eighty-four-year-old woman. Each movement seemed a burden. She was frail and hunched, a tiny woman, shorter perhaps than anyone I had seen in the temple court, and yet she shuttled about with purpose, lending her support to whomever was in need. Her object at the moment was a crippled man sitting near the gate. Indicating the crippled man, Simeon explained, "The man to whom Anna is giving service was born mute and deaf. In his youth, his legs were crushed under a wagon. His friends bring him here daily to the temple to beg. He has no other means of support. His meals consist of that which people give him."

Suddenly uncomfortable, I placed a hand on my purse as if to protect it. Impatiently, I said, "I must be going. Surely you know a generous vendor here."

Simeon appeared disappointed. He gestured toward a table beyond the crippled man where a vendor sat selling sacrificial birds in wicker cages. Simeon said, "That is the man you seek." Before I could hurry away, he grabbed my arm and said, "You are so anxious to obey the letter of the law that you miss the point: sacrifice has nothing to do with animals; sacrifice has everything to do with the heart. The greatest sacrifice is *you*, Joshua; it is charity. And when you can make that sacrifice, it empowers you and sets you free." Then regarding me, he added, "But charity requires great faith." Simeon smiled and released his grip. Bowing slightly, he bid me farewell, saying, "Go in peace, Joshua ben Levi."

I thanked Simeon, turned to depart, and then stopped short.

"What is the matter?" Simeon asked.

I did not know. As I gazed alternately at the cripple and the vendor, I began to feel uneasy. I asked, "You say the crippled man has no support?" Simeon nodded. I turned my attention again to the crippled man, and as I gazed upon him, I suddenly felt small and ashamed. I knew what Miriam would do in this situation. She had never done an unselfish thing in her life. I looked at Simeon. "You are right. It takes so much faith."

He placed a hand on my shoulder. "It is when you let go of the rope that you fall into the safe arms of God. That is the great discovery of life." Then as if to lead me, he asked, "Wasn't your purpose a turtledove and a prayer?"

I smiled and thanked him. "You have helped me decide what I must do." Then in parting, I said, "I hope you find your Messiah."

Simeon embraced me and whispered reassurance, "I come here every day seeking him, and I am never disappointed."

"I don't understand," I said.

Simeon gestured toward the crippled man. "I find him whenever I serve his children." Simeon paused. "Perhaps in that way you will find him, too."

With that, we parted, and I made my way through the crowd toward the crippled man. As I drew near, he lifted his head in anticipation. I judged him to be about the age of my father and yet somehow he appeared much older. His clothes were worn to the point of being immodest, his legs twisted awkwardly beneath him.

He raised his cup to me with a shaky hand and begged for money. I noticed that the cup contained only two mites, the smallest coin in the Empire. As I considered him, I remembered Miriam's charity in similar situations. Her reaction to being childless was to reach out to others. Once, she labored all day to cook a delicious meal. I discovered the feast that evening when I returned from the fields. I was famished, and when I smelled the food, I hurried to sample it. But when I lifted the lid of a boiling pot, Miriam goodheartedly cracked my knuckles with a spoon, as if I were a naughty child. She informed me that the food was for a weary mother whose four children were abed, sick with fevers.

That had not been the first time I'd gone hungry while Miriam served others. I became used to watching her leave our home in the early evening, carrying hearty meals to those in need. I had never begrudged Miriam her avocation, but that evening certainly tried my patience. When I complained, she handed me one of the pots and two loaves of fresh bread and ordered me to help her convey the meal to the sick family. Reluctantly, I obeyed her.

When we delivered the meal, the mother broke down and cried. Seldom had I seen such need and such gratitude. My hunger fled, and my body filled with feelings of empathy and love. That night I gained a new appreciation for my tenderhearted wife; I finally realized why Miriam seemed driven to do such things. Giving love was nourishment to her. She did not consider love a mere feeling; to Miriam love was her reason for living. That night I gratefully shared a plain meal with my sweet wife. It was perhaps the most satisfying meal I ever enjoyed.

Now, looking at the crippled man, I tried to see him through Miriam's eyes. I could not imagine such a life: the constant embarrassment of begging day after day, the sum purpose of his existence to procure food for his next meal. Deaf, he could hear no sounds of love or laughter; mute, he could not communicate his innermost feelings; and crippled, he had to depend on the kindnesses of others to move from place to place. I wondered what kept him alive.

I knew what Miriam would do. I knelt beside him and emptied my purse into his cup. Now the two mites became seven, and his response to his good fortune was tears of gratitude. He reached out and grasped my hand and nodded a gesture of thanks, as if I had just handed him a treasure. I had seldom received such an expression of gratitude.

"There is no need to thank me," I said. Remembering his handicaps, I found myself struggling to communicate, mouthing each word deliberately.

I felt a hand on my shoulder and looked up. Anna, the old woman whom I had observed assisting the man, stood above me. "Let me help you communicate with him," she offered.

"Thank you," I replied. "I wanted to tell him that he is . . . my brother. That is why I gave him the money. There is no need to thank me."

Anna smiled and made motions to the man. He turned and looked at me with apparent understanding. He set down his cup and took my hands in both of his. In some remarkable manner, we communicated. Thinking of Miriam's charity again, I looked up at Anna and asked, "Is he hungry?"

"He is always hungry," she replied.

I reached for the scrip that hung about my tunic. It contained a few morsels of food for my journey. I handed it to the man, embarrassed that it was so little. To Anna I said, "Tell him I am fasting today. I won't be needing the food."

Anna obliged, and the man began to eat the food hastily. Then Anna knelt beside me and said, "A fast yields no blessing unless you serve someone. May God bless you with what you fast for today."

We watched the man enjoy the food as if it were a fine feast. When he finished, I stood to leave. The man gazed at me with great love as if he would ask me to stay. As if he could hear me, I said, "I really must go." Something in his expression told me that he understood. He squeezed my hand again then made a gesture that I could not decipher.

Anna helped me. "He is blessing you," she said. I felt suddenly warm. Now I knew why Miriam was constantly searching for someone to serve. If it was possible, I loved her more at this moment than I had ever loved her in my life.

I left Anna and the crippled man. I had just let go of the rope, and I prayed that God would catch me. Now I would have to go to the temple and approach God with no sacrifice except that of a broken heart. That was everything that I had to offer when I would pray for Miriam in the Holy Place. All I carried with me now was the gratitude of Rebekah and her son and the thanks and blessing of my new brother.

Chapter 5

HERE I RAISE MY EBENEZER

I climbed fourteen steps, passed through the Beautiful Gate, and entered the Court of the Women, the first area of the inner temple compound. I noticed many people within the court worshipping in humble reverence or coming out of or going into the four large rooms at each corner. I crossed the marble floor eastward and headed toward a massive bronze door, the Gate of Nicanor, which led into the sacred inner courts where the great altar of sacrifice stood in front of the temple. I climbed fifteen more steps and entered the Court of the Men. In this narrow courtyard, I could observe the sacrifices being made on the altar in the innermost Court of the Priests, and beyond it, the holy temple.

The area was crowded, but not as much as the outer courts. I moved to a far corner, and there I prepared to plead with God for Miriam's life. My heart was heavy with grief and anxiety. The weight of my burden pressed down on me so that every movement that I made seemed an exertion.

I prepared to pray, strapping my small, leathern

phylacteries to my left arm and forehead, and then lifted my prayer shawl. I paused and considered its workmanship. Miriam had sewn it for me as a wedding present, "to abide under the shadow of the Almighty," according to the psalmist. On the day of our marriage, we covenanted to live in the safety of obedience, under the watchful care for God. Now, in reverence, I draped the prayer shawl over my head, and prepared to offer up the prayer of my life. But I could not even utter the first word.

As I looked out upon the great altar of sacrifice, the fear returned that without a sacrifice, my prayer might fall short. I mourned that I had nothing to offer—nothing except my broken heart. I removed the prayer shawl from my head and looked toward the temple for courage. Twice a day a white cloud of incense would issue from the top of the temple and rise heavenward to God carrying the prayers of Israel. I longed that my prayer might likewise ascend to the Almighty.

I broke from my thoughts as a father and his young son walked past me. The father was instructing his son in the ordinances of the temple. Pointing to the altar, he said, "It is constructed of unhewn stones, as tall as three men, rising fifteen cubits into the air." Then he indicated the rampart that led to the altar's summit. Priests were ascending and descending with animal and meal sacrifices to place on the fire that burned on the uppermost surface.

The boy said, "It seems so cruel."

The father said, "The law of sacrifice helps us remember that a price must be paid for every broken law." When he said no more, I assumed that he was like most Israelites, who possessed a thin knowledge of their religion. On the other hand, my father had taught me that the law of sacrifice was profoundly sacred and rich in symbolism. The sacrifice of something valuable requires great faith, my father had said, and it is faith coupled with sacrifice that draws down the blessings of heaven and opens the door to reconciliation with God.

The father turned to me and began to apologize. "I am sorry if we disturbed you. My son is a son of the law now. This is his first visit to the temple."

I smiled and addressed the boy. "Then you are *bar mitzvah*."

The boy nodded, "Yes, I am a son of the law."

"What is your name?"

"Daniel."

"I am Joshua. Have you come to make a sacrifice?"

"Yes. This is my first time." Daniel indicated a lamb that was tied to his wrist with a cord. "I raised him from a newborn."

"I can only imagine that your sacrifice will be very difficult for you," I said, the image of Amit flashing through my mind.

The boy nodded and looked to his father anxiously. The father put a hand on Daniel's shoulder and turned to me. He introduced himself. "I am Rafael. We have come from Jericho for Passover."

"You have come before the rush?" I asked.

"Yes, and to visit family here in Jerusalem."

"I live in Beit Sahour," I said.

"A shepherd."

"Yes." I looked at Daniel then back to his father and said, "You have taught your son well." Rafael thanked me and I turned to Daniel and asked, "What will you do when you make your sacrifice?"

"One must confess his sins before proceeding," he said, as if reading from the Talmud.

"That is right," I affirmed. "But I doubt that you have committed any grievous transgression."

"He is very obedient," his father said proudly. At that moment, considering the prayer that I needed to offer, I recalled every sin, however minute, as it passed before my mind's eye. Suddenly, I felt a great desire to confess every misstep that I had ever taken. I felt the heavy burden of careless actions, things left undone, and I hoped that God would be merciful and overlook them.

I said to Daniel, "Do you see the people as they bring their animals to the priests to be sacrificed?" Daniel nodded. "They lay their hands on the head of the sacrificial animal with their whole force. They are transferring their identity and offences to the substitute. Do you know why?"

The boy answered, "They sacrifice the animal to represent the death of their old way of life." I felt a pang of conscience at Daniel's answer.

Rafael seemed pleased with his son's answer. He asked Daniel, "And having paid such a price, would you ever return to your old way?"

Daniel knelt beside his lamb and held him. "No, I could not."

We watched the people render their sacrificed animals. They would return to their homes and eat everything, nothing wasted, to represent internalizing their new sinless way of life. Observing the scene, Daniel said, "It is 'an atonement for your souls,'" quoting Moses, who had explained the necessity of sacrifice. At that moment, I yearned to become "at one" with God. I knew that only a full partnership with the God of heaven could produce the miracle that I sought at His hands for Miriam.

"Will you excuse me?" I said, indicating my prayer shawl, "I have come to pray."

"You have no lamb?" asked Daniel.

His father shushed him and began to apologize.

"It's all right," I said. Then to Daniel, "I did have a lamb, but—" I hesitated, an explanation would take much too much time. "—this time my heart will have to do." Daniel grew serious, apparently pondering my words. I turned to his father and said, "I really must be going."

As I turned to leave, Daniel said, "'To obey is better than sacrifice.'"

I stopped short.

The boy continued, "Those are the words of the prophet." He quoted another verse: "'The sacrifices of God are a broken spirit: a broken and a contrite heart.'"

I bent toward him. "What are you saying?"

He looked at me then, as though he suddenly understood the weight of my burden. He said, "God will surely accept your sacrifice. I am certain that He will bless you today."

I embraced him and began to weep. His father said, "Daniel is a good and truthful boy."

As I held Daniel, I said, "Thank you, Daniel. Thank you for your blessing." Mere moments ago we had met as strangers; we became friends; now we were departing as brothers.

I moved to a more secluded place, placed the prayer shawl upon my head, and prepared again to pray. I pictured Miriam the last time I had seen her. I had held her hand as she fought for her life, a dead child in her womb. I had brushed back the damp hair from her face, wishing that I could convey to her the deep feelings in my heart. If love were the salve of healing, I could have healed her at that moment. Looking into her exhausted eyes, I had feared that I would lose her, and if that happened, I didn't know what I would do. I couldn't imagine life without her. When she squeezed my hand and sent me on this journey of faith, she looked at me pleadingly, and said, "I believe in you, Joshua. I believe that you can ask God and he will hear you. God will bless us today."

I felt my inadequacy keenly, and once more I began to weep, turning my face from any curious onlooker. I knew myself. I was neither strong nor composed of superior faith. I had no special dispensation with God to gain his ear and his grace. I was only a poor shepherd. Beyond my immediate family and the few people who lived in my little village, no one would ever know my story. Why should the great God of the universe stoop to pay any mind to someone as flawed and as weak as I?

I dried my eyes, and, gazing up at the House of the Lord, I drew in a deep breath and spoke: "O God, I have no lamb; I have no dove. I stand before thee empty-handed. All I have to offer thee for Miriam's life is my heart, and it is broken. I pray that thou will overlook my weakness and save my wife because of *her* faith. O God of Abraham, Isaac, and Jacob, I beg thee to likewise spare my wife as thou saved Isaac at the point of death. O God of Moses, I beseech thee to likewise deliver Miriam, as thou delivered the children of Israel. O God of Daniel, I implore thee to likewise rescue my wife from death, whose mouth gapes as wide as a lion's to devour her. O God of my father, Levi, whom thou has always loved and supported, bless too my sweet Miriam with thy healing love."

I could think of nothing else to say. I grieved that I had neither the faith of my father nor of Miriam. Surely my prayer had been too weak to surmount the skies and penetrate the realms of heaven and persuade God to intervene. I was not a man of eloquent speech; I did not know how to pray with better language. Now my wife's life was seeping from her like ice melting in the warmth of morning, and the only thing that stood between her and the grave was my poor prayer.

I departed the temple feeling unsure and woefully inadequate. Questions invaded my mind: Did I really know God well enough to petition Him? Did He really have ears to hear my cry? If He had heard me, was Miriam's condition too hard for Him? And finally, did He love me enough to help?

I exited the city with these questions following me like a shadow. Evening was giving way to night now. To cut time and to avoid the crush of travelers flowing into Jerusalem from Bethlehem, I chose to take my chances by traveling overland through the rough terrain that separated me from Shepherds Field and Beit Sahour. When the sun had fully set and the horizon had migrated from the color of milk to black, a feeling of apprehension settled upon me. I encountered no living thing in this wilderness. I had never felt so utterly alone. The darkness enveloped me with a feeling of dread; it was as silent as an arrow flying toward my heart.

I lit a torch and prayed that I might find my way home and that Miriam would still be alive. That was all that I dared hope for. I had no path to follow, but I knew the way. I hurried over stones and crags, the toes of my feet bloody from the jagged rocks and the jabbing brush. My legs and lungs began to burn. Most of the day I had either been walking or running, and now my legs were betraying me. That I had not eaten today did not help. My energy waned. Only focusing on Miriam provided me strength to continue.

As I hurried, I recalled Simeon asking me if I had noticed a new star in the east. I afforded myself a brief luxury by glancing heavenward, but the glow from my torch obscured the view. If the star was up there, tonight would have been a good night to see it, I thought. The sky was unusually clear. Nevertheless, I doubted the old man. I imagined that his ability to prophesy was as potent as my ability to pray and receive an answer. On other nights, tending the flock, I had enjoyed gazing at the stars. I had seen wondrous sights—stars shooting across the sky, and the sun and moon disappearing in each other's shadows.

I had been taught miraculous stories of the earth standing still or retreating at prophets' commands, but I had never known the universe to spawn a new orb. As everyone knew, the foundational lights in the heavens were static. They had to be. We measured time and seasons by them. We counted on their constant predictability. Any disruption in heavenly movements and formations would have profound cosmic significance and turn our world on end. Such a breach of the normal order would surely mean the judgment of God was upon us, the implications of which I could not imagine.

I arrived at the meadow near Beit Sahour winded and weak. I could see the area easily now. The moon had finally risen, large and yellow, aiding me on the final leg of my journey. I found the sheep safely folded for the night. My fellow shepherds had herded them into the mouth of a cave and sealed the entrance with a barrier of stones and thorny bushes to keep the sheep in and the predators out. My father was standing sentinel at the entrance of the sheepfold. When he recognized me, he dropped his staff and rushed toward me. "Joshua!" he shouted. The other shepherds heard his cry, abandoned their occupations, and hurried in my direction. My father embraced me and said, "I have worried about you."

"I am fine," I said. Grasping his arms, I ventured, "Have you received any news from home?"

He hesitated.

"Father?"

He shook his head slowly. "It is not good."

I felt my body begin to fail. Two shepherds stepped forward to steady me. I said to my father, "You don't mean—?"

"Sit down, Joshua."

My father tried to steer me towards a large rock, but I collapsed on the ground and began to sob. I doubled over and drew my hands in close. My mind scrambled for meaning. My father knelt beside me and held me. Finally, when I could speak, I asked, "Are you saying that Miriam is dead?"

"We don't know . . . we think so." His speech was soft and laced with emotion. It was then that I noticed Ephraim, the eight-year-old son of Reuben. The small boy approached tentatively. My father put a hand on the boy's shoulder and said, "It's all right, Ephraim. Tell Joshua what Leah said."

A shy boy, Ephraim hesitated to respond. Reuben knelt beside his son to encourage him. "Don't be afraid," he said. "Tell Joshua what you saw and heard." Ephraim shook his head and buried it in his father's shoulder. Reuben looked up at me sadly and then spoke for the boy. "Miriam took a bad turn, Joshua. We think she may be gone by now."

Tears spilled down my face. I looked at my father for verification, and he nodded. I searched the shepherds' faces and found all of them weeping. I pulled Ephraim into my arms. Tears were streaming down his cheeks like rivers. He wrapped his arms around my neck and his little body shook. I whispered, "Tell me what happened, Ephraim."

With a faint voice, he said, "I went to your home with my mother. She and the women were helping Miriam. Suddenly, they began to cry. Some of the women were screaming. Leah told me to run . . . run to the shepherds and find you. . . ." Ephraim choked on his words and could not continue.

"Did you see—?" As much as I tried, I couldn't bring myself to ask the question. I drew a deep breath and tried again. "Did you see Miriam . . . die?" The little boy clung to my neck and cried. "It's all right," I urged him. "You can tell me."

After a long moment, he uttered a weak, "There was so much blood."

I stood then and began to sob. My father tried to comfort me, but I was unwilling to be consoled. "You should go home, Joshua," he said.

"Go home? Go home to what?" I removed the turban from my head and threw it upon the ground, as if the turban were my faith. I collapsed to my knees and ripped my tunic from the neck to the waist. Taking a handful of earth I poured it upon my head, wailing as if I had been cast into the bowels of hell. All the shepherds, including my father, began to weep bitterly. I threw back my head and howled.

Then I stood and forsook the company, sprinting toward the hillside overlooking the meadow below. I climbed, weeping, my chest heaving, clawing my way to the top. Arriving at the summit, I threw myself prostrate onto the ground, only then realizing I was beside my father's Ebenezer.

I wanted to accuse God. How could He abandon me? How could He take from me she who was most precious to me? Where was the loving, compassionate, all-knowing, all-powerful Being whom Israel claimed to be the one true God? Something inside of me wanted to strike back at Him, and yet some unseen thing tethered me to Him as if to draw me closer. I breathed hard and wept, momentarily disconnected as though I were an observer watching the two forces within me struggle for prominence. Exhausted, I rolled onto my back, wiped my eyes, and stared up at the swath of stars, which looked as though someone had spilled gems onto the floor of heaven.

My life with Miriam began to play out before my eyes. I pictured our childhood, our betrothal, and our marriage. Oh, how I had loved this woman! We had grown up together in marriage. I envisioned our joy and hope at the news of her first pregnancy, and I remembered our bitter disappointment when the baby within her had died. I saw the scene play out yet again, when once again she conceived and lost the child. Through it all, Miriam and I had grown closer; as close, I imagined, as any two people could. Our hearts beat as one. I could not draw a breath without sensing that she breathed with me in rhythm. Three times daily, as was the custom, I had knelt before God to pray, and the first words out of my mouth had always been words of gratitude for His blessing me with Miriam. Would God take her from me? Had He already? Could I go on?

Lying beside my father's Ebenezer, I remembered his experience here on the day of my birth, when he had lost my mother. After he completed this monument, he had planted his feet firmly upon the ground and shouted out his allegiance to God. Now, here I was in a similar situation. Earlier today, my father had asked me if I, too, could declare my allegiance if the worst were to happen. I could not answer him then, an admission that had shamed me. But now the moment had arrived. I asked myself if I was willing to shrink and make a mockery of my faith. Was I willing to cast aside the foundation of my beliefs and declare the substance of my life a lie?

I thought of the prophets and their difficult lives. They were considered great men of God because they had endured extraordinary abuse and privation while maintaining their integrity. It was the depth of their suffering and the breadth of their devotion that made their teachings valid. I realized that if I were ever to become a man of God, like my father, and if I were to become comfortable in the company of prophets, I, too, had to press through my adversity and be willing to cry my allegiance to my God.

I stood upon my feet with purpose. Summoning courage, I began to survey my father's Ebenezer—his "stone of help." Every rock that comprised his monument was a declaration of his faith and trust in God. What's more, each stone was an affirmation of his love for the Lord. What had he told me earlier? "This is the place where God helped me that day."

I knew what I must do. Pushing through the profound sorrow that I felt for the loss of my wife, I thrust my hand into the earth, and with great determination pried loose a large stone until it yielded and broke free. I hefted it to my chest, pressed it high over my head, and set it squarely on the top of the Ebenezer. Standing back, I raised both arms toward heaven, and cried out, "I will never leave thee! I will ever trust thee! Nothing could cause me to forsake thee, my God!"

Abruptly, I felt the earth move beneath me, as though it had suddenly become liquid. I steadied myself with a hand on the monument, while something akin to a tremor reverberated through the air. It hit me as hard as if it had been the blast of a trumpet, but I heard no sound. Then, as unexpectedly as the quake had occurred, everything became absolutely still, as completely silent as one might experience deep in the belly of a cave. Nothing moved. No breeze, no far-off sound of sheep bleating, no noise of crickets or other nightlife. Nothing. I was only aware of the rapid beating of my heart. I did not move; I did not breathe.

As though it had been a spectacular strike of lightning, a blinding light burst forth from heaven and flooded Shepherds Field. Instantly everything became brighter than midday. The light pierced the darkness of night like the first dazzling rays of morning, immediately eclipsing the light of the moon and the stars. It was unlike any other light that I had experienced. The light struck me with such force that I found myself lying on my back staring heavenward, unable to move, my strength having fled.

The light felt amazingly tangible; it entered my body with the same sensation as coming in from the cold and downing a warm drink. The light seemed to seep into every fiber of my soul until my entire body was warmed and *enlightened* by it.

The light dispelled every particle of darkness in my being, and its warmth seemed to cleanse me; its presence seemed to wash away impurities, and its brightness burned out every doubt. If love were a substance, then this light was love, for it filled me with the most profound assurance of celestial affection and enveloped me as with a holy embrace.

As I gazed into the light, I beheld a glorious being standing above me—an angel from the presence of God. His countenance was brilliant. If it were possible, his body appeared brighter than the light that surrounded him. In fact, I could see that he was his own source of light; it radiated from him as though he were the sun. Nevertheless, his brilliance surpassed that of the sun, which in comparison would have appeared as a dim planet. Somehow I became aware that every particle of his body was vividly alive in a way that it could perceive and communicate truth.

He was dressed in a robe of the most exquisite whiteness, a golden sash girded around the middle and tied on the side. His dress could have been that of a priest, except that his head was bare, as were his feet and hands. He had a white beard the color of crystalline snow in the blazing sun, and his equally white hair flowed down over his shoulders in waves. His skin was not flesh-colored, but radiant white and as clear as amber, almost transparent, and his eyes were as a flame of fire. In every way, the angel was a being of glorious light, as splendid a specimen of manhood as I could ever have imagined.

My first reaction was fear; not frightened fear, but holy fear, a profound sensation of reverence, awe, and respect. The angel gently bent toward me and gestured with his hand, as would a friend. "Fear not," he said, and when he did so, a thrill of hope shot through my body like lightning. His voice was mild and harmless, yet it was commanding. Although it was soft, it trumpeted a message of grand import. His words issued from his mouth like the sound of rushing water, making my voice sound coarse, weak, and primitive in comparison.

Though the angel spoke in my language, I perceived his communication more in my mind, and that caused me to struggle to attune my ears to his message. I was suddenly impressed with divine proximity; God was near. The feeling carried with it complete awareness, concern, and, remarkably, familiarity. I could not remember feeling so safe or so well known. I sensed that nothing could happen to me that heaven could not repair, that all would be well, no matter what happened.

As I gazed into the light surrounding this holy being, the thought struck me that I was perceiving *glory*—the visible manifestation of divine presence, the ancient glory of the Lord that had always signaled his nearness. It was the *Shekinah*, the brilliant pillar of light that had rested upon the Holy of Holies in the Tabernacle as our fathers had sojourned in the wilderness, following Moses to the promised land. This glory of the Lord had departed Israel hundreds of years before in the days of Ezekiel because of wickedness, and ever since the people had mourned its loss. But now, tonight, the ancient glory had returned, signaling the fact that the light of God was once again coming to the earth.

I became suddenly aware that this glorious light was sustaining me in a manner that allowed me to behold the angel and endure his presence. Amazingly, as the light filled and washed over my body, I felt *enlightened*, and somehow I knew more. Principles that had evaded me now seemed clear, and questions that had haunted me now vanished. My mind was fully open; the light poured into it without resistance or restriction, filling me with intelligence and truth. Moreover, each of my senses was heightened and on fire: I could see more, hear more, smell more, feel more, and understand and love more.

By the act of merely speaking, the angel's presence

seemed to search me, and I was suddenly aware of every misdeed that I had ever committed that had distanced me from my God. Now more than ever, I yearned for reconciliation, and I had no desire to do or think evil. I only wanted to bask in this love and remain in the divine presence forever. No price seemed too great to pay.

At the angel's first words, I recognized that I was about to hear something singular. I glanced down upon the meadow below and noted that my father and the other shepherds were experiencing this same vision. When I turned back to behold the angel, he continued with his message: "Behold, I bring you good tidings of great joy, which shall be to all people. For unto you is born this day in the city of David a Saviour, which is Christ the Lord."

Could it be? The promised Savior, the Messiah, had been born today in Bethlehem? Since the world began, all the prophets had foretold this event, and now it had happened? But why tell us? We were but lowly shepherds, the poorest of society, a hiss and a byword among the people. Why not proclaim the news to the leaders of the venerable Sanhedrin? Why not tell them that the promise of the ages, the glory of Israel, had finally come to *all* people! Why not proclaim the news in the courts of emperors? The King of kings is born today!

Then the angel said, "And this shall be a sign unto you: Ye shall find the babe wrapped in swaddling clothes, lying in a manger."

My astonishment could not be contained. *Lying in a manger?* Where livestock feed?

Just as I was trying to comprehend the irony of the King of kings having been born in the low condition of a stable and lying now in a harsh manger, the heavens exploded with myriad angels, who filled the sky from horizon to horizon, as deep and as wide as I could see. Their numbers eclipsed the multitude of visible stars on a clear night. It was as though every inhabitant of the celestial realm could not be restrained from bursting through the veil of heaven to shout the greatest news that had ever been revealed to men on earth.

The angels' voices rang from one end of heaven to the other—a magnificent chorus, perfectly blended as if they were one voice, praising God for His goodness, mercy, and grace. Some angels blew trumpets; others played harps, pipes, timbrels, psalteries, and cymbals. The angels shouted the prophecies of the Savior's birth, His coming mission, and His eventual triumph over death and sin. They sang of His love and power and glory. They rejoiced that men could now be reconciled with God, and that every knee would one day bow and every tongue confess that this child was indeed the promised Christ, that He alone had power to wipe away all tears and heal and help, and that He would humble the proud and exalt the poor and purify His people as if with fire.

As I gazed awestruck at the celestial scene, I again marveled that we poor shepherds should be so privileged. I was astonished that above us in the heavens, angelic men and women, the hosts of heaven, could not be held back. They had burst from their realms of glory to proclaim this astounding event, and for some unapparent reason, God had chosen us to receive the news.

With a grand crescendo, the angels united their voices in a magnificent finale: *"Glory to God in the highest, and on earth peace, good will toward men!"* Their song seared itself into my mind. The melody was uncharacteristic of Hebrew harmony; neither did I believe that it could issue from man's genius. The music was wholly unique and celestial in quality, and it carried a message that I would never forget.

Chapter 6

FOR UNTO US A
CHILD IS BORN!

I rejoined my companions and found them engaged in astonished conversation. *Who could understand the full import of the vision? Why had the angel made the annunciation to us?* They stood huddled in a tight clutch, their lamps lit, the night having returned to darkness now. My father sat cross-legged near the group, speechless, his head bowed. As I drew close and put a hand on his shoulder, he lifted his head. His face was pale and tear-stained. I perceived that he was too weak to stand.

"Father?" I knelt beside him.

He looked at me with an expression that I had never seen. In a whisper he asked, "Did you see the angel? Did you hear the hosts of heaven singing?"

"Yes," I answered.

"Then it is true. The Messiah is born in Bethlehem, just as the prophets had foretold." The other shepherds drew nearer and joined in his rejoicing. Reuben bent toward him and asked, "Can you stand, Levi?"

My father answered, "I think so."

Reuben gestured to the others and said, "Help me lift him." Gently, they raised my father to his feet. When he was standing, he gazed up into the sky, spread his arms toward heaven and cried out Isaiah's prophecy: "For unto us a child is born, unto us a son is given: and the government shall be upon his shoulder: and his name shall be called Wonderful, Counsellor, the mighty God, The everlasting Father, The Prince of Peace."

As with one voice, we all shouted our rejoicings. We could not hold back. It seemed as if every particle of our being was on fire and demanded a voice to cry out the news. We gloried in the prophecies concerning the Savior. We shouted, *"Hosanna! Hosanna, to the Most High God!"* We sang the exultation that we had heard the angels sing: *"Glory to God in the highest, and on earth peace, good will toward men."* But the message that continued to resonate within me was the angel's first declaration, "Fear not." Those words echoed in my mind. I now found it impossible to harbor anxiety or despair. To my father I said, "We must do as the angel directed."

He nodded and grasped me by the shoulders. "Yes." His strength had returned. "Let us now go even unto Bethlehem, and see this thing which is come to pass, which the Lord hath made known unto us."

As we started for Bethlehem, little Ephraim, Reuben's son, asked timidly, "Should I stay with the sheep?"

We halted and looked at each other as if to search for an answer. Never had we left our flock unattended and vulnerable to predators. As we contemplated Ephraim's question, we felt a sense of calm envelop us. Reuben knelt beside his son and drew him close. "The sheep will be safe," he assured him. "Another Shepherd will watch over them tonight. You must come with us, my son, for you too are a witness."

The thought astounded me: *We were witnesses!* Nevertheless, I sympathized with Ephraim. As much as he felt concern for the flock, I had felt concern for my wife. When I had left her this morning, I had felt that I was abandoning her. Now, as I considered postponing my return home where my wife lay dying or dead, I felt a sharp pang of conscience. Was I doing right? As I pondered the question, the feeling of guilt dissipated like smoke rising in the air; I felt only peace and remarkably a sense of purpose. Somehow I felt that I would find my answers in Bethlehem, and I knew that I must be obedient to the angel's directive to go and find the Child.

One of the shepherds asked, "Where shall we go? The angel said we would find the Babe lying in a manger. But there are many caves and khans in and about Bethlehem.

How will we find Him?" My father smiled knowingly. The questioning shepherd looked at him and asked, "Do you know where we should look, Levi?"

My father answered by quoting the ancient prophecy of Micah: "And thou, O tower of the flock, the stronghold of the daughter of Zion, unto thee shall it come, even the first dominion; the kingdom shall come to the daughter of Jerusalem."

Astounded, I said, "We will find the Child at Migdal Eder?"

My father nodded, and as he did, I felt my mind open and light began to pour into it. *Migdal Eder!* I looked up into the eastern sky. There, in breathtaking view stood a gleaming new star, just as Simeon had foretold. I had never beheld it before. It glistened in majestic splendor, glowing like a bright beacon, eclipsing the brilliance of the morning star that heralded each new day. I had never beheld its equal. I was about to draw attention to the wonder when I heard the shepherds excitedly buzzing, "Migdal Eder! Migdal Eder! The Messiah has been born at the Watchtower of the Flock!"

Seeking clarification, I asked my father, "Are you certain that we will not find the Messiah in the manger of a khan?"

He shook his head and affirmed, "No, we shall find him at Migdal Eder."

I knew the location well; every local shepherd did. Migdal Eder was an ancient place situated on a high hill at the north end of Bethlehem on the road to Jerusalem. Its name literally meant "the watchtower of the flock." In ancient times, it had been built as a military tower to survey the environs of Bethlehem in an effort to protect the city. Our forefather Jacob had journeyed to Migdal Eder with his flocks, when his wife, Rachel, began hard labor and died giving birth to Benjamin, my ancestor. Mourning bitterly, Jacob built a tomb in Bethlehem and buried Rachel in it. Still in tears, Jacob pitched his tent at Migdal Eder, where later the sacrificial lambs would be born, and still later, where the special Lamb would one day be born to comfort Jacob and his children.

From those early days until the present, shepherds had employed the high watchtower and the cave over which it was built to defend and protect Israel's sheep from enemies and wild beasts. When the temple had been rebuilt and sacrificial ordinances were renewed in it, this sheltering tower and its cave became a special place where shepherds such as us often brought their birthing ewes that belonged to the temple flocks. My companions and I were the most recent shepherds in a long line who cared for the lambs born at the Watchtower of the Flock, lambs whose destiny was to provide an atonement for the sins of the people. Because our charge was singular, we operated under strict rabbinical rule to maintain Migdal Eder as a ceremonially clean stable for birthing the lambs of God. When the lambs were born, we would swaddle them in special cloth to protect them from injury. Now, according to my father, we would also find the Lamb of God wrapped in swaddling clothes and lying in a manger at the Watchtower of the Flock.

My father said, "God, through his prophet Micah, gave us a sign seven hundred years ago, predicting where the Messiah would be born. The Savior will come to the tower of the flock, and that place shall become His first dominion."

I knew that many rabbis had taught that the Messiah would be announced from Migdal Eder in Bethlehem, and apparently it was so. I rejoiced with the shepherds. God could not have chosen a more fitting location. The Messiah had not been born in the filthy stable of a khan where travelers' smelly cattle and donkeys were kept. No, the Lamb of God had been born in Bethlehem at the traditional birthing place of the sacrificial lambs— the actual location where tens of thousands of lambs of God had been born, prefiguring Him. We shepherds, who had always been the first to witness and receive the announcement of a birth of a lamb of God, were now the ones to witness and receive the first announcement of the birth of *the* Lamb of God.

We hurried to Migdal Eder as if on the wings of angels, rejoicing and singing praises. Each of us conveyed a lamb as a gift, which was the tradition of shepherds. As we ran, we cried out the prophecies concerning this Child. One shepherd shouted, *"This is our God; we have waited for Him, and He will save us."* Another cried, *"The people walking in darkness have seen a great light. He will open the blind eyes to bring out the prisoners from the prison."* I immediately thought of the glory of the Lord that we had beheld. I wondered had all Israel seen it too? When we arrived, would we be among tens of thousands who had also seen the light and had come to see the newborn king?

My father began to sing the prophecy of Isaiah like a psalm: *"He shall feed his flock like a shepherd: he shall gather the lambs with his arm, and carry them in his bosom, and shall gently lead those that are with young."* Suddenly, I loved my profession more than I ever had before; to be a good shepherd exemplified the Messiah's mission.

We arrived at Migdal Eder after midnight. An exulting procession, we were as the rejoicing friends of the bridegroom having finally come for his bride. Now we stood before the Watchtower of the Flock. It was an ancient structure that showed its age and yet was functional and kept in good repair by the shepherds. It stood tall on a high hillside overlooking Bethlehem and the surrounding area. A circular stone tower, the watchtower boasted four levels of windows, each level higher than the last, allowing a shepherd to climb up and peer out in any direction.

The watchtower had a flat, walled top, and its base was as rocky as a stone quarry. I scanned the immediate area and noted that we were alone. I saw no parade of people pouring out of Bethlehem or Jerusalem to see the newborn King—only we poor shepherds. My father was the first to stoop down and reverently enter the cave over which the tower was built.

The large cavity was dark except for a dimly lit area at a far corner behind a shrouded, makeshift curtain. In the darkness I could barely make out the various birthing stalls and some of the implements that we used in our profession. The area was as clean as one could make a cave, but it was empty now that lambing season had ended some weeks earlier. Only one Lamb had remained to be born.

Suddenly, we heard a tiny whimper, which was

followed by the soft singing of a young woman. Then there was movement. My father hushed us, and we remained absolutely still, not knowing how to proceed. Within a few moments, an older woman emerged from behind the curtain carrying an armload of linen—a mid-wife, I presumed. She seemed startled when she saw us. She quickly stepped back behind the curtain and then reappeared with a young man. From across the cave in the dimness of lamplight, I could not make out his features, except that he was head and shoulders taller than the woman. The lambs we were carrying became restless and bleated. My father took a step forward and called out to the young man, "Peace be with you. We are friends. We have brought gifts for the Child."

The young man stood still as if he were considering my father's greeting. Then he turned and said something to the older woman. With that, she moved towards us carrying her bundle, and passed us by with an acknowl-edging smile and nod. When she had exited the cave, the young man stuck his head behind the curtain, spoke quietly, and reemerged. As he approached us he bowed and said, "Peace be with you. Have you traveled far?"

I was struck with his gracious demeanor. Standing now in the glow of our lamplight, he came into focus. He was about my height, but a few years younger, I judged.

He might have been the age I was when Miriam and I had wed. He wore an earthen-colored tunic. Glancing beyond him, I noticed the curtain partitioning off the cave for privacy, and I surmised that it was his cloak.

The young man's facial expression and his speech were most congenial, and he offered his smile generously. He wore a dark, neatly trimmed beard, his eyes were black, and his complexion was olive. I could see by his build that his trade required him to work with his hands and body, but because he carried neither rod nor staff, I guessed that his profession was not that of a shepherd. His Galilean accent betrayed him. Men from that province were known to be workers of stone, wood, and metal.

My father offered a slight bow and said, "I am Levi, and these are my companions. We are shepherds from Beit Sahour."

The young man bowed in return and introduced himself. "I am Joseph, son of Heli. My wife, Mary, and I are from Nazareth in Galilee, and indeed she has borne a son this night. Will you come with me to see him?"

Joseph's invitation caused my heart to pound hard. As we moved toward the curtain carrying the lambs in our arms, I struggled to control my breathing. Joseph parted the curtain and we entered a tiny area that had served as one of the birthing stalls for ewes. The stone walls seemed to be a harsh backdrop for the holy scene that opened before my eyes. There, in the warm glow of lamplight, lying on a makeshift bed of straw, covered by a blanket, was a young woman of the most exquisite beauty. Except for my Miriam, I had never encountered such loveliness.

She was exceedingly fair and white, uncommon for Judeans. She was as delicate as a rose petal or the whisper of a breeze. Her stunning beauty caused me to halt in temporary paralysis. I remained awestruck and motionless as I gazed at her, and as I did, an impression flowed into my mind that recalled the words of Isaiah: *"Behold, a virgin shall conceive, and bear a son, and shall call his name Immanuel."*

I beheld the young woman in silent wonder. Here was a mother who had just given birth, and yet in truth I knew that somehow she was yet a virgin. An impossibility! But then again, every miracle bears witness of its Author. Clearly, this miracle doubled as evidence of the power of God and a sign of the Messiah's birth. As I stared at the young virgin mother, I imagined that others might judge her to be nothing more than a lovely peasant girl, and yet in every way she was a royal princess, a precious and chosen vessel, the mother of Immanuel, meaning "God is with us."

A manger stood before the young mother, a limestone feeding trough hollowed out and lined with straw. There, lying in the manger, was a tiny infant. He was wrapped in crimson swaddling clothes, a red square of cloth with long ribbons to hold the Child's arms and legs straight. Because the symbol of a lion was prominently stitched into the swaddling cloth, I assumed that the couple descended from the tribe of Judah through the lineage of David.

We stood in hushed reverence, gazing at the Babe. As I looked at him, the psalmist's question came into my mind: *"Who is this king of glory?"* And the words of the prophet provided an answer: *"I will raise unto David a righteous Branch, and a King shall reign and prosper, and shall execute judgment and justice in the earth. In his days Judah shall be saved, and Israel shall dwell safely; and this is his name whereby he shall be called, THE LORD OUR RIGHTEOUSNESS."*

Suddenly, my father set aside his lamb and fell on his face, prostrating himself before the Child, weeping openly. "Thank you," he said through tears. "Thank you for coming to me when my wife died. Thank you for walking beside me all these years, for talking with me during the dark and lonely times, for teaching me, and for comforting me. You are my most cherished friend. I love you." He began to weep uncontrollably, no longer able to speak.

I could not hold back my tears. I had never seen my father affected so. I looked about me and noticed that all the shepherds were weeping, as were Joseph and Mary. Then Reuben approached the Babe in the manger and gazed at Him with profound adoration. Reuben tried to form words, but his effort failed him. It was as though this giant of a man had suddenly been reduced in stature to that of a little child in the presence of this Babe. Reuben began to weep, and all of us wept with him. At length, he dried his eyes, drew a deep breath, and declared, "Thou art truly the Messiah!"

When Reuben had said this, he turned and motioned for his son, Ephraim, to come and see the Child. Ephraim, who had been standing beside me, clung to my tunic. I bent down and met his eyes. "It's all right, Ephraim," I said. "Go and see the Child."

Slowly Ephraim walked to his father and knelt before the manger. He stared at the Babe and then looked up at Mary, who smiled at him. "Have you seen a newborn baby before?" she asked.

Ephraim nodded. "Yes, but I have never seen a king."

"How did you come to find us here?" she asked him.

"The angel told us."

Mary looked up at Joseph in apparent astonishment, but then they seemed to understand and smiled at each other. Turning back to Ephraim, she asked, "What did the angel say?"

"'Fear not . . .'" Ephraim began.

At this, Mary's eyes welled with tears.

"Thank you," she said. "You could not have brought us a finer gift."

One by one, each shepherd drew near to the Child, presented their lambs as gifts, and worshipped him. I alone stood back and watched the scene, trying to assimilate all that was happening and everything that had occurred that day. As I observed this little family, I could not help but imagine a similar scene, had the events been different. My Miriam could easily have been Mary, cradling a newborn son in her arms. I could easily have been Joseph, proudly entertaining guests who had come to admire our child. As I gazed at Mary with her beauty and tender demeanor, I began to mourn: *How shall I ever go on without my Miriam?*

As my heart filled with sadness, Joseph stepped toward me. Putting an arm around my shoulder, he said, "I perceive that you have come with a heavy heart, my brother. Let me take you to Him." I stared into Joseph's gentle, encouraging face and began to weep. He held me in his strong arms as though we were longtime friends. Without shame, I heaved great sobs as I clung to him. He whispered, "You have been carrying your burden alone for too long. Let us help you."

With that, Joseph guided me toward the manger, and as he did the shepherds drew back. I knelt before the Child and gazed into His perfect face. I had never beheld anything so beautiful and mild. His eyes closed, and as they did, Mary asked, "Are you married?"

"Yes," I answered softly. "Her name is Miriam."

"Like mine," Mary responded, for her name was a derivative. Then she added, "She must be lovely."

I nodded. Then looking at Mary, who reminded me so much of my wife, I replied, "Miriam is beautiful."

"And do you have children?" she asked.

I shook my head. "Our child died recently."

Joseph put a hand on my shoulder. He and Mary looked at each other as if to communicate with their eyes. She smiled at him. Turning to me she asked, "Would you like to hold Him?"

I began to protest. "Oh, I don't think I could—"

Joseph knelt beside me. "It's all right."

Mary reached into the manger and tenderly lifted the tiny bundle into her arms. "Make a cradle of your arms," she instructed me. Joseph demonstrated the position. When I had knit my arms together, Mary gently set the Child in them.

The Baby was so very small, as light as lamb's wool. His tiny eyes, nose, ears, and mouth were perfectly formed. His skin was the color of milk and as smooth as soft butter. He had a hint of light-colored hair that lay flat against His head. He remained very still in my arms. I brought Him close to my ear and listened to His breathing, quick like a bird's. I kissed Him tenderly on the cheek, and as I did, He opened His eyes and whimpered. I looked at Mary and began to apologize, "I'm sorry. What shall I do?"

"Rock Him and sing to Him," Mary replied patiently.

I surveyed the shepherds for help but found none. What song do you sing to a king? Ephraim seemed to know. Quietly, he began to hum a familiar melody—the song that the angels had sung tonight. Then Ephraim began to sing the words: *"Glory to God in the highest, and on earth peace, good will toward men."* Ephraim did not sing the song as had the angels: a great anthem of exultation. Rather, he sang it softly, like a lullaby. The song filled me with great emotion.

I looked into the face of the King of kings and began to sing softly to Him the song that the angels had sung to us—the shepherd's song. While I sang and rocked the Child, He calmed and gazed up into my face, His eyes penetrating me. I studied His features, and a sense of familiarity entered my mind and heart. I knew Him! I had seen Him in every person I had encountered today. Rebekah and her son, the family headed for Jerusalem, Simeon, Anna, the crippled man, and the father and son in the temple.

An expression of gratitude seemed to emanate from the Child: *Thank you for blessing my children.* I had never experienced the feeling of reverence as I did in that moment.

I thought to myself, "I am looking into the face of God! I am witnessing what righteous men and women have longed to see and did not. I am one of the first to behold the Lord's salvation."

I thought of the words of the prophet: "*Mine eyes have seen the king, the Lord of Hosts.*" That realization flooded my mind with other prophecies my father had taught me about this Child, the mission of His life, and what He would yet suffer for me: "*He is brought as a lamb to the slaughter . . . Surely he hath borne our griefs, and carried our sorrows . . . He was wounded for our transgressions, he was bruised for our iniquities . . . and with his stripes we are healed.*"

As I gazed at Him, I felt as though He spoke to my mind: *"I was wounded in the house of my friends . . . I gave my back to the smiters . . . [and] hid not my face from shame and spitting. They pierced my hands and my feet."* This communication caused me to shudder, for I suddenly realized that if I had been the only person who had ever been born, He would have willingly come to earth to suffer and give His life to rescue me. Now, because He was here, I knew that He would provide me a way to escape all my troubles. I would no longer be held captive by my mistakes; I could learn from them without being destroyed by them. Then the words of the prophet pierced my heart: *"He hath poured out his soul unto death: . . . and he bare the sin of many."*

As I gazed adoringly into the Child's eyes, a feeling of recognition settled upon me. Astonished, I felt as though the room had emptied and that I was completely alone with Him. All sounds seemed to cease except for the beating of our two hearts. The angel's words echoed in my mind: *"Fear not!"*

I looked at the Babe and said, "Thank you for my life. Thank you for giving me Miriam. You have always loved me and overlooked my weaknesses. I know that you will always love me and never leave me, and because I know that, I need never be afraid." When I had said this, the words of the prophet Isaiah flowed into my mind as if the Child were confirming their validity: *"He will swallow up death in victory."*

Knowing this, I realized that my life would never again be the same.

Chapter 7

THE SHEPHERD'S SONG

We departed the Watchtower of the Flock, glorifying and praising God for all the things that we had both seen and heard. I looked up toward the eastern sky and saw the new star shining brilliantly. I pointed to it and rehearsed to my companions everything that Simeon had told me earlier in the temple. How I wished he could have been with us tonight! But I knew that the Lord had promised him he would live to see the Christ. My heart took comfort that Simeon's faith would soon be rewarded.

We came to a crossroads on the path leading to Shepherds Field. There we stopped, and each of the shepherds embraced me, lending their support. One more task remained, and each of them seemed to sense how difficult my returning home would be. My father asked, "Do you want me to go with you? You shouldn't be alone."

I considered his offer and then slowly shook my head. "I will not be alone," I said. "I can do this now."

My father hugged me and said, "Believe, Joshua. No matter where your journey leads you, there is no risk in trusting God."

I did not run home. Strangely, I felt no need. I walked, contemplating the situation that I was about to find. Despite the prospect of my wife's death, I clung to my declaration of allegiance to God that I had made earlier tonight. After all that had occurred, how could I ever blame God recklessly or take an action that might distance me from Him? Nevertheless, I felt profound sorrow when I imagined life without Miriam. As I walked the distance home, I tried to steel myself against the wave of grief that would surely crash upon me when I stepped through the door.

I walked by the light of a shepherd's lamp, which gave light to my feet. When my father had traveled his road of sorrow, his faith had given light to his feet. I marveled that he could suffer the loss of his wife and yet trust God as he pressed forward. Where had that ability come from? I remembered that tonight he had spoken to the Child as if he were speaking with his dearest friend. My father had paid a high price for that relationship. I wondered if I, too, was willing to pay such a price. Earlier, I had cried my allegiance to God. Could I do so now?

My question was about to be answered.

The streets of Beit Sahour were empty and dark as I approached my home. A thick silence had settled on the little village, and a heavy apprehension weighed upon me. The courage that I had summoned faltered. No enemy is as certain or as cruel as death. It broods about us with gaping jaws, ready to devour young or old with no courtesy of timeliness or sensitivity. To defeat this monster was the work of God. In death's presence no man had power. As I drew near my home, I heard someone crying. I held my lamp higher and saw the silhouette of a woman sitting outside the door, her hands to her face. I hurried toward her. She looked up at me with a tear-stained face. *Leah!*

Astonished at seeing me, she cried, "Joshua! Where have you been? Oh, Joshua!" My mother-in-law stood as if to embrace me, but terror seized me. I pushed past her and burst through the door. There I beheld my worst fear: an empty bed covered with blood-stained linen. My knees buckled and I crumpled to the floor, weeping. The strength that I had tried to summon fled entirely now. Miriam was my life! I could not draw a breath without thinking of her. I could not remember a time when I had not known her. She was the beginning and the end of every day. Without her, my life held no purpose. I held my face in my hands and rocked, wailing and sobbing.

Leah rushed to me and enveloped me in her arms. "It's all right, Joshua," she tried to comfort me.

"No," I cried. "It can never be all right."

"But it *is* all right," she insisted.

Then I heard a sound that I had long hoped to hear but dared not imagine: the sound of a tiny cry. A voice spoke my name: "Joshua." I turned. There in the corner, in the dim lamplight, sat my Miriam . . . rocking a baby! She said, "You have a fine son."

Stunned, I looked at Leah for confirmation, and she smiled and nodded. "It is a miracle, Joshua," she said, beginning to cry again. "God gave us a son tonight. Go and see him."

Astounded, I moved toward my wife, unable to reconcile the information that was flooding my mind. I knelt beside her and stared at her, then at our child, and then at Miriam again. I surveyed her face, checking every detail against the memory of her in my mind. Was I dreaming? My questions were coming faster than I could form them. Miriam took my hand and placed it on her cheek. "It is true, Joshua. I am alive." Then she placed my hand on the child. "And so is your son." What she said next caused tears to spill from my eyes again: "God heard your prayer, and He has blessed us today."

I gazed at her with wonder. She was beautiful. Her smooth, olive complexion appeared healthy and vibrant now. Her soft chestnut hair was washed and combed so that it cascaded down over her shoulders. I took her delicate hand in mine and traced its petite bones. I kissed it gently as she whispered, "Is anything too hard for the Lord?"

I shook my head. "Not for Immanuel."

She looked puzzled.

I responded, "Now I know that God is with us indeed."

As much as I had cried during the day, I thought I could summon no more tears. But I was wrong. When I looked at my son, his dark eyes open and peering at me, I could not contain my emotions. I wept unashamedly. The tears seemed to wash me clean of all the pain I had carried. I felt joy fill me with the same warmth I had felt when the glory of the Lord had rested upon me.

I gazed at the child—*my child!* He was so small and delicate. His tiny features were flawless in every way. His complexion reminded me of his mother's, as did his nose and mouth. His hair was soft like lamb's wool, about the color of mine. Miriam had wrapped the child in a swaddling cloth that she had embroidered with symbols that represented our family's lineage and our tradition of shepherding. In forty days we would present him to God in the temple, where we would offer a lamb to symbolically redeem him. Perhaps we would meet Simeon there. That was a fond hope.

"Would you like to hold your son?" Miriam asked me. I dried my eyes and nodded. "Make a cradle of your arms," she said. I knew how. She gently placed the tiny bundle in my arms.

The child lay still and stared up at me. I brought my ear close and listened to his breathing. Then I kissed him tenderly on the cheek and thanked God silently. Still looking at him, I began to ask my wife, "How did—?"

Leah completed my question. "—this happen?"

"Yes, tell me."

Leah knelt beside me and stroked the child's head. "We were losing Miriam," she began. "She had lost so much blood. I sent Ephraim to find you, but you had left for Jerusalem already. We feared that Miriam would not survive the hour. When we drew the child from her, he was not breathing. We worked with Miriam when she cried out suddenly, and her heart ceased to beat. When all seemed lost, something amazing happened." Leah paused as if she were searching to find the right words.

"What happened?" I urged her.

"Something brilliant like lightning illuminated the sky, and suddenly the child gasped for breath. At that same moment, Miriam opened her eyes and began to cry." Then Leah asked, "Did you see a great light tonight, Joshua?"

I smiled.

Miriam looked at me questioningly, and asked, "What was it?"

I answered, "The Light has indeed come to earth." Miriam's expression showed that she did not understand. I explained, "The Messiah has come, Miriam. He was born this night in Bethlehem. I have seen Him." Then I understood. I looked at my son and said, "When the Messiah drew His first breath, our son drew his."

Leah's expression was that of sudden realization. Excitedly, she announced, "When the light shot across the sky, an impression shot through my mind, as though it had been a voice. It said: *Fear not!*"

I completed the angel's message for her: "For, behold, I bring you good tidings of great joy, which shall be to all people. For unto you is born this day in the city of David a Saviour, which is Christ the Lord."

"Do you know what the saying means?" she asked.

"It means that we need never fear," I replied.

The baby began to whimper, and Miriam reached for him. I said, "Let me. I know what to do. I know how to calm little—" I hesitated a moment and looked to Miriam for help.

"*Joshua,*" she said. "Just as we planned, we shall call him after his father: Joshua—*Jehovah is salvation.*"

I smiled. "I know how to calm little Joshua. I will rock him and sing to him."

"What will you sing?" she asked.

I knew the answer. Bending close to my child, I began to softly hum the angelic melody. He quieted immediately. I stood and walked him to a window and looked out. There in the eastern sky stood the brilliant star beaming with promise. I turned and gazed at my wife, beautiful, radiant, smiling at me adoringly. I cuddled my son in my arms and looked deeply into his face, alive, vibrant, and perfect in every way. My heart overflowed with gratitude. Once more, tears flowed freely.

How do you thank someone for giving you back your wife and blessing you with a son? Standing in the warmth of my home amongst my family, I knew that I had come to the end of a long journey; I felt as though I had entered my promised land.

Miriam had been right: God had indeed blessed us today. I gazed up at the star. Cradling my son, I pointed toward it and whispered to him softly. He stared at me with shining eyes, and I imagined that he understood. Something miraculous had happened tonight, and the world—*our world*—would never be the same.

I held my child and again began to hum. I was not a singer, but I sang to him just the same. It was the song the angels sang to us from the heavens: *"Glory to God in the highest, and on earth peace, good will toward men."*